BOOKS BY AVA STRONG

REMI LAURENT FBI SUSPENSE THRILLER

THE DEATH CODE (Book #1)
THE MURDER CODE (Book #2)
THE MALICE CODE (Book #3)
THE VENGEANCE CODE (Book #4)
THE DECEPTION CODE (Book #5)
THE SEDUCTION CODE (Book #6)

ILSE BECK FBI SUSPENSE THRILLER

NOT LIKE US (Book #1)
NOT LIKE HE SEEMED (Book #2)
NOT LIKE YESTERDAY (Book #3)
NOT LIKE THIS (Book #4)
NOT LIKE SHE THOUGHT (Book #5)
NOT LIKE BEFORE (Book #6)
NOT LIKE NORMAL (Book #7)

STELLA FALL PSYCHOLOGICAL SUSPENSE THRILLER

HIS OTHER WIFE (Book #1)
HIS OTHER LIE (Book #2)
HIS OTHER SECRET (Book #3)
HIS OTHER MISTRESS (Book #4)
HIS OTHER LIFE (Book #5)
HIS OTHER TRUTH (Book #6)

CHAPTER ONE

Light exploded in Mauro's eyes, lancing through his retinas into his brain. His confused, pounding brain. Blinking painfully, he clambered from his prone position on the thick woolen rug, to teeter on his hands and knees.

Man, this had been a party. A part-ay! Another wave of dizziness struck, and he slumped down again, the wool soft on his cheek. The unforgiving glare of the morning sun through the large window was too much to bear. It felt like his head was going to explode. What had they been drinking?

He'd lost count after the eighth gold tequila. That stuff had been nectar. Poisonous, evil nectar, as it happened. His stomach churned at the memory. Had he thrown up? If he had, he must have been somewhere else at the time, because the rug looked fine. How embarrassing would it have been to have woken in a pool of his own vomit, in this fancy house?

Raising his head again, peering across the enormous lounge, he noticed that the large front door stood open. Beyond it, he heard retching from somewhere outside, and his own stomach flip-flopped in uneasy sympathy.

"Alain?" he called. "Is that you?"

Where was his friend? He needed him for the ride home. Had Alain left without him? Feeling anxious now, Mauro sat up. Memories flashed through his mind. They'd played dares at one stage. Right here in the lounge. He guessed that's where a lot of the damage he felt now had been done. Mauro never refused a dare. Ever!

The weird memory of doing a body shot off of some babe's tanned, slinky stomach surfaced suddenly. He remembered smooth, golden flesh, the gleam of a navel ring, the tequila burning a well-traveled path down his throat, the appreciative roars of his friends.

Jeez!

Looking around, Mauro saw to his concern that the place was trashed.

On arrival, he and Alain had been astonished at the size and scale of the swanky venue to which they'd been invited. Well, not exactly invited. To which a friend of a friend had said they should come along, because there was a big bash, and everyone was welcome, and the drink was free and flowing. And it had been. His memories were hazy, but he remembered it had felt like an extremely classy hotel.

Now, it was wrecked.

The reason the light was so bright was that the window glass was broken. Through the giant, shattered hole in the enormous picture window, the cold morning sun glared at him like an accusing eye. Glass was scattered over the carpet. He was lucky he hadn't passed out in the heaps of fragments, he thought uneasily. He could have cut himself.

He checked his hands, but they looked fine. They were shaking, though.

Then, staring around, he took in the scale of the destruction.

A giant red stain dominated the pristine cream carpet. A smashed wine bottle lay nearby, the likely culprit. Beyond, it looked as if someone had dropped a massive tray of snacks and then fallen on them. Well, that could have happened. Melted ice-cream, squashed buns, lurid yellow mustard and pink ketchup created a crazy modern art effect on the half of the carpet that had escaped the wine catastrophe.

One of the cream chairs lay on its side, its cushion ripped half off. Another had its leg broken. One of the paintings on the walls was ripped clear through, all the way to the backing and there were a few holes, actual holes, in the surrounding plaster. Dimly, Mauro remembered that had been the result of a complicated dare involving beer bottles. At the time, they hadn't seen the holes, because an earlier perfect score had shattered almost all the bulbs in the overhead chandelier, which now listed to one side.

His heart was pounding faster. This was crazy, insane beyond any quick fix. He needed to get out of here before someone responsible realized what had gone down. This looked as if a gang had broken in.

For one hopeful moment, Mauro entertained the possibility that a gang had, in fact, broken in.

He shook his head, a movement he instantly regretted as the sharp, throbbing pain intensified. And then, his gaze landed on a shape in the corner that distracted him from his misery.

"Alain? Alain!" Mauro staggered to his feet, grinning widely at the sight of his friend, who'd managed to pass out with his arms around his head and his butt sticking straight up in the air. How'd he done that? A snort of laughter burst from Mauro's dry lips. That was some accomplishment.

By a miracle, his phone had survived the night in his zip-up jacket pocket. Mauro actually fumbled it out, planning to capture this embarrassing moment, before logic caught up. Having a photographic record of anything in this house would be a dumb idea. They needed to hotfoot it out of here.

If Alain could actually hotfoot it anywhere. A rush of fear drenched the spark of amusement he'd felt.

Alain wasn't moving. What if something had gone wrong, like he'd choked on vomit or bashed his head? He looked still. Weirdly, impossibly still.

Mauro was starting to worry that this crazy, wild night might have had terrible consequences.

"Hey, Al? Al?" he called softly.

There was no movement. His friend didn't appear to be breathing at all.

"Al!" Frantically, Mauro grabbed his shoulder and shook it hard. "Al! You okay? Talk to me. You okay?"

Slowly, inexorably, Alain tipped over out of his unlikely semi-crouch. He toppled sideways, landing with a bump on the thick carpet.

He was blinking, Mauro saw with ineffable relief. Blinking as if the incoming light was a weapon.

"Hey," he groaned, his voice hoarse. He scrambled to his feet and stared around him.

"We need to get out of here," he said, reaching the same conclusion Mauro had done, a lot quicker.

"Yeah, we do. We do, but we need to clean up first," Mauro said.

His jacket stank of raw whisky and his hair was matted with ketchup. The red wine that stained the carpet had also found its way across Alain's shirt, which was smeared with mustard. He wasn't sure either of them was in any state to drive, but most definitely, they needed to clean up before arriving back at the university residence.

His phone buzzed. Peering at the screen, reality hit Mauro like a cold shock.

"We've got soccer practice in an hour. We need to leave, now. Coach Jacobs and the guys will be waiting. We're going to be in huge trouble with the team if we're late. And we can't arrive looking like this. They'll ask where we've been."

Mauro had seen how Coach Jacobs dealt with players who arrived late, hungover, or still drunk for practice. He'd never thought he'd be one of them, until this morning.

They staggered, zombie-like, across the room.

Alain was in a panic.

"I'm sure someone already called the police. I can hear a car outside," he hissed, causing Mauro's heart to accelerate.

The hallway was littered in beer bottles, a few of which had smashed onto the tiles. Crossing it hurriedly, Mauro skidded and almost fell as he slipped in a pool of beer.

"Here's the guest bathroom." Eagerly, Mauro wrenched open the door and, just as fast, slammed it shut as the reek of vomit rushed out.

"It doesn't look good in there," he mumbled, his own gorge rising again.

"Okay, it's a big house. There'll be a lot more bathrooms," Alain encouraged.

"We don't have time!" Mauro agonized. This was his worst nightmare made real. If the police didn't get them before they left, their coach would get them when they arrived back.

They rushed further down the corridor, wrenching open the next bathroom door. There, two sprawled, snoring girls effectively blocked the way between the door and the sink.

"I think I hear another car," Alain said in a tense voice as they rushed on.

"This whole place is a destruction zone," Mauro said.

"I really hear a car," Alain sounded panicked. "For real, this time. I can hear the tires rattling over paving. It's going to be the police arriving. I'm telling you."

This could be bad. There could be big trouble. Mauro was almost twenty-one. Just a few more months to go. But if the police saw him now, they would have clear evidence that he'd been breaking the law.

It would mean trouble with his parents back home in Chile. It could even mean the end of his student visa and he didn't want to think what they would say about that.

"The master bedroom. Let's go there. It's at the end of the corridor," Alain said, sounding relieved.

"Why there?" Mauro asked, hustling after him.

"Because that guy last night said nobody must go in there. I guess they were keeping it clean, being the folks' room."

Given the state of the rest of the house, Mauro didn't think the folks were going to be grateful. But he also didn't think a quick wash-up in their bathroom would make things any worse.

They reached the door and Mauro opened it.

He stared in awe at the massive room beyond. The gigantic four-poster bed was draped in cream and gold with a massive, plush headboard. Exquisite furniture – a settee, an ottoman, a vanity with a small, delicate chair – completed the ensemble.

"I hear voices," Alain implored. "Someone's here. I'm telling you!"

Quickly, they tiptoed to the side window and peered out.

Mauro couldn't see the driveway, but relief filled him as he saw that what he'd thought was a giant window was in fact a glass sliding door which for some reason was unlocked and partway open. So after a lightning wash-up, they could get out that way and run through the grounds, down the driveway, and all the way to the road where Alain's ancient Ford was parked.

Putting the curtain back in place, Mauro hurried past the enormous dressing room to the bathroom door.

"Let's get cleaned up and go," he said, feeling as if his plan might just save them both. If they were really quick, they'd be in time for coaching. If he was lucky, he wouldn't throw up halfway through.

"Something in here doesn't smell so good," Alain said, sounding worried.

Mauro couldn't smell anything over the fetid reek from his own shirt.

Dunking it in the tub would be the best idea, he decided. There was a huge sunken tub in the corner of the bathroom with a curtain drawn partway across it.

He hurried over and drew the curtain back.

And there she was.

Staring back at him through wide, unseeing, bloodshot eyes.

Her mouth was open, her lips drained of color. Her swollen tongue lolled from between them, and her face was bloated and greenish white. Limp strands of blond hair hung over the rim of the tub.

Amid the sound of his own panicked yelling, the high-pitched shrieking of pure terror, which was echoed by Alain, he took in the impossible sight.

A corpse in the bathtub, sprawled and dead.

A corpse. A dead body.

This wasn't possible, it was not real, it must be some kind of practical joke, there couldn't be a dead woman here. As he stared in dismay, a dizzy blackness threatened to envelop him, and his knees buckled alarmingly.

Then Alain grabbed his arm, jolting him out of it.

Forgetting the need to clean up, they made a panicked dash for the glass door, shouting in horror as they burst out and raced across the lawn

Mauro didn’t care anymore what trouble they might be running toward.

All he cared about was getting far, far away from the puffy, lifeless face with its gaping lips, which would haunt his nightmares for years to come.

CHAPTER TWO

Stella Fall stopped the rental car and then hastily jammed it into Park as her shaking foot slid right off the brake. The slam of the car door sounded loud in the silence. It was quiet up here in the mountains. The silence felt vast, impenetrable.

She was riding on a wave of adrenaline. All her senses were heightened as she stood, gazing at the small, wooden house. It was set in a ramshackle, but cared for, garden, and dwarfed by the pine forest behind. On either side, the mountains soared. The small town of Ouray was cradled in a scenic valley between the craggy peaks of the San Juan range.

Finally, she had arrived at her father's last known address.

One day, when Stella was ten, her father had gone to work, traveling from the dilapidated farmhouse where they lived, into the Kansas police precinct where he worked as a detective.

He'd never come home again.

The agonizing, lonely days of 'missing' had passed, and hope had faded as 'presumed dead' became the most likely outcome and, eventually, the official verdict. But Stella had always felt, with an irrational certainty, that her father was still alive.

She had sat in his workshop in the afternoons, looking at the well-worn but well-kept woodworking tools he'd used, wishing for his quiet, strong companionship and support, because without his tempering influence, the storms of her mother's rage were even more destructive.

Then her mother had cleaned out the workshop, sold the tools, and locked up the room that had been her refuge. As time had gone by, her fading memories had been all she'd had, until her surprise discovery.

Just a few weeks ago, unpacking old boxes, she'd found a postcard, sent from Colorado after his disappearance. Stella had gone straight to Kansas to confront her mother. That trip had been a conflict-filled waste of time, but since then, surprisingly, Rhonda Fall had relented and Stella had received a message back with this address – 5 Wilderness Avenue, Ouray, Colorado.

Now, she was here to search for George Caleb Fall, and unlock the mysteries surrounding his disappearance.

In her wallet, she'd stashed one of the rare photographs she had of herself with her dad.

Stella had inherited her ice-blue eyes and dark hair from her mother. Those strong, intense genes had overpowered her father's brown hair and hazel eyes and kind, softer features. But she hoped beyond words that she'd inherited his calmness and balance, his quiet, humble approach, rather than the blazing storms of her mother's personality.

This seemed like a humble house. A place where he would have been happy to live.

Her heart accelerated as she saw the car parked in the drive. The elderly Buick signaled someone was home. She'd never allowed herself to go as far as visualizing the car her father might drive if he was still alive, but if she had, it would have been something like this.

Stella swallowed down her nerves. There was no more time to think or delay. The reckoning had arrived.

She strode up to the house and tapped on the front door.

She waited, her mouth dry, her ears straining as soft footsteps approached. Emotions clashed within her, hope warring with fear.

The door opened and she stared into the surprised eyes of a gray-haired woman, short and plump. She had flour on her hands and was wearing an apron.

From inside the house, Stella smelled the warm, rich fragrance of baking bread.

"Morning. Can I help you?" she asked curiously.

"I – I'm Stella Fall." To her dismay, she found she hadn't rehearsed what to say or how to handle this moment. Now that it had arrived, and her father hadn't opened the door, she felt adrift.

"I'm looking for a man called George Fall. He's my father, in fact," she admitted. "I believe this was his last known address."

The woman's face pinched in incredulity, but to Stella's relief, she didn't seem put off by this weird sounding introduction.

"Your father? He lived here? How long ago was that?"

"Sixteen years," Stella admitted.

The woman frowned. "We've only been here five years. My husband bought this place when we retired. Before that, I know it was a deceased estate for a while."

Stella's heart clenched. Deceased estate? Surely this couldn't be?

"Do you know who the previous owner was?"

The woman shook her head. “My husband dealt with that side. All I know was that it complicated things and slowed down the sale. And my husband is away now. He’s in Silverton for the day.”

Stella stared at her pleadingly as her hopes and dreams crashed around her. Eventually, the woman spoke again.

“I know who’d know. Jeff next door. They’re long-term residents, been here for twenty years or more. And I don’t think they’ve left for the church social yet.” She pointed to the small home, fifty yards down the road. “If you hurry, they’ll be there.”

“Thank you,” Stella said.

She rushed down the road, skidding on the patch of ice on the sidewalk. It was bitterly cold, although until she felt the ice under her shoes, she hadn’t noticed it.

She knocked on the door of house number 4, and a moment later, a lean, tanned man with an unruly mop of white hair opened it.

He was dressed in a smart jacket and black pants, at odds with his ramshackle appearance, and was carrying a plate of sandwiches. Clearly, he was heading out.

“Good morning,” Stella said in a rush. “I’m sorry to interrupt your Sunday. The neighbors said you might know about a previous resident of their home. I’m trying to trace him. His name’s George Fall, and he lived here about fifteen years ago.”

Not daring to breathe, she waited for the dreaded news that her father was dead.

“Good morning,” the man said slowly, looking Stella up and down in a rather critical way, as if her haste had bypassed important social niceties. “Well, this is a surprise.”

He paused. He glanced at her, and then at his sandwiches, as if reminding himself that the trip to church took priority.

“There’s never been a George living in that house,” he explained firmly.

Stella felt as if the rug had been ripped from her. Her first, immediate, unwanted assumption was that her mother had lied.

Was it possible?

With Rhonda, nothing was impossible. It was well within the bounds of possibility that Rhonda could have sent her on a fruitless search, providing a random wrong address, just to taunt her daughter.

But for Rhonda, that would be out of character, Stella revised. Her mother had always gotten immediate results with her hurtful words, her mood swings and insults and screams. She liked to be there to watch the pain they caused. Not for Stella to be hundreds of miles away.

"Are you sure?" she asked.

Luckily, he didn't take offense, but simply interpreted it as a request for further detail.

"The couple next door has been there a few years. Before that, Hamish Brand owned it. Hamish died in his nineties and the place stood empty for a while after that while his estate was wrapped up."

Stella felt a rush of relief so vast that it was dizzying. It hadn't been her father who had died.

"And before that?"

"Well, Hamish owned the home for many years. He let it out to folks before he moved in himself," the man said, sounding perplexed.

"Who was the tenant before Hamish moved in?" Stella asked.

"We're talking more than ten years ago?" the man confirmed. "At that time, Frank lived here a few years."

Frank?

"Frank Newman," the man added.

At first the name meant nothing to Stella. But then, the last name started to prickle her instincts.

Newman. New man?

A new name. New life. Was it possible her father had assumed a false name? This was a truly weird and unexpected twist, but then, so much of what her father had done had been out of character for the man she knew.

"What do you remember about Frank?" she asked, hoping for more detail.

"Quiet guy. Kept to himself. He was in his late forties, I guess. He did some odd jobs for people in town while he was here. Very good with his hands. He actually made our post box, and the board fence in our front yard," he pointed. "Well made. Thirteen years old, and it looks like new. All we do is oil it every couple of years."

Stella's conviction solidified. This had to be her father. Had to be.

"Where did he go?"

Jeff shrugged. "He moved out one day and wasn't here anymore. I don't even think anyone wondered where he'd gone. This is a vacation town. People come and go."

"His phone number. Did you ever call him?" Stella asked.

"Now, that's interesting. After he left, I did try calling his number a few times. I wanted to know if he'd help with a few more woodworking projects in the spring. But it was out of service and has stayed that way. I'll give it to you if you like, but I can tell you now, it won't be answered."

"Please give it to me anyway," Stella said. Thinking of other avenues, she tried, "Did he have any friends in town? Did he attend any clubs, or church, or bars?"

Jeff smiled wryly. "Frank and I would share a beer at the bar from time to time, but I never saw him sitting with friends. He didn't attend any of the socials in town. He wasn't a talkative person. I think we were the people who knew him best, and my wife and I barely knew him at all."

Stella felt confused all over again by this information. Her father hadn't kept to himself. He'd been well liked at work, and on friendly terms with the neighbors. The George Fall she remembered would have ended up helping organize the town's socials, not avoiding them.

He'd changed, Stella realized, and wondered if she would ever know the reasons why.

Jeff looked at Stella more closely, and she saw sympathy in his eyes.

"You really want to find him. This is important to you, right?"

"It is," she said miserably.

This trip was proving to be a dead end. Her father had lived here. He'd come and gone. Nobody knew him and nobody had gotten close.

What had been going on, she wondered, feeling a sense of helplessness that her efforts were too little, too late.

"Write down your number for me," Jeff said. "I have to get to church now, but I'll send you the last number I had for him as soon as I've gotten home and found it in the old address book. And I'll do some talking and asking on your behalf. I know a couple of the folks he did jobs for. I can find out if they still hear from him. If there's any information, I'll let you know."

"Thank you," Stella said. She wrote her number down for him, feeling once again that it was better to stay under the radar, and that this was definitely not the time to hand over her FBI card.

"Have a good day," he said cheerily.

As she left, Stella turned to look at the split-pole fence. The boards were fitted together neatly and carefully. The fence was well constructed. The post box – large enough for newspapers and small parcels – was beautifully made with a quaint little handle on the door.

Her father's work. Precise and tidy. As opposed to her father's life, which Stella feared was a mess that would never be resolved.

Climbing into her rental car, she felt depressed that she'd gotten nowhere and that her journey here had been a waste of time.

But Stella then comforted herself with the thought that it hadn't. She'd found out he was here for some years. His presence in the town, though fleeting, had touched some people's lives. Someone might still have a tenuous contact with him.

Before she headed off, her phone beeped.

Glancing down at the screen, Stella felt her new life, her real life, take center stage over her exploration into the past.

Special Agent Roth, the boss at the New Haven FBI office, had messaged her.

"Fall, a new murder case has just come in. You and Maxwell will be handling it. We need to meet ASAP so I can brief you. Thanks, R."

Stella reread the message in amazement. She and her investigation partner Maxwell were being handed full responsibility for a brand-new case. A murder investigation, no less.

Going solo was a big and important step for both of them. And a murder was likely to be a difficult and complex case. They were both relatively new agents. She'd been with the Bureau only a couple of months, and Maxwell had just a year's experience. Why had Roth decided to hand them this responsibility?

Stella felt eager to know what their first solo case involved.

CHAPTER THREE

The next morning, at a quarter to six, Stella arrived at the FBI New Haven office feeling anxious. Roth had wanted to meet as soon as possible. She'd explained she was out of town and would only arrive home after midnight, so he'd scheduled the briefing for the early morning.

Stella had barely slept, knowing that every minute counted, and worrying that she was already compromising the success of this case.

She climbed out of her small Ford Fiesta at exactly the same time Rick Maxwell, her investigation partner, climbed out of his low-slung Mustang.

"Well, hey! You also got the memo about the meeting?" the fit, dark-haired Maxwell asked, a grin warming his tanned face.

"That's a surprise! Maybe Roth sent it to the whole department?" Stella quipped back, and they laughed. The humor made her feel better. It eased the pressure she felt about handling this new case.

In fact, it wasn't just the laughter that warmed Stella. Simply being in Maxwell's presence was enough to lift her spirits, making her feel motivated to do her best, and be her best. Suddenly, the dark, chilly predawn seemed brighter.

The young, dynamic, ferociously intelligent Maxwell had been partnered with her for the past few cases they'd investigated. Although he'd started out resenting her the first time she'd been involved, things had changed a lot since then, and in surprising ways.

Stella wasn't ready to classify her feelings as romance yet. Both of them were taking it slow. But, as they headed toward the main entrance, she felt a flash of warmth as his hand accidentally brushed hers.

Quickly, she walked ahead as they entered the main building. The security guard on duty at the door nodded politely as they hurried through. Even at this early hour, New Haven was bustling with activity. Mondays were always busy. The spacious lobby resounded with the trilling of phones, the muted chatter of voices, and the tapping of footsteps on the gleaming tiles.

The clean, distinct smell of polish had become a familiar scent to Stella as she entered the building.

They turned down the corridor where Roth had his offices. Striding alongside her again, Maxwell checked his watch.

"We're early. Want coffee?"

"Thanks, I'd love some," Stella said gratefully.

Maxwell peeled off, heading for the kitchenette, and Stella walked into the office.

She saw Roth's laptop open on the desk. So he was here. A moment later, he appeared, talking on his phone and holding a bunch of papers. His chestnut-brown hair, although freshly cut, looked as if he'd slept on it wrong. Stella had often thought with some amusement since joining the team, that despite Roth's incredible skills and leadership, every day was a bad hair day for her boss.

"Yes. Yes. Absolutely," he said into the phone. "I'm about to meet with my agents. They'll be on the scene in a couple of hours." He disconnected and put the papers down on his desk. "Morning, Fall. Morning, Maxwell," he said, as Maxwell rushed in with three steaming cups.

"I'm sorry I couldn't meet yesterday," Stella said, feeling guilty all over again that she'd chosen the wrong time to explore her father's past.

"The local police made a start on it," Roth reassured her. "However, it now means we need to move fast. We can't afford any further delays."

They sat down at Roth's desk.

"Okay. First things upfront. For this murder case, you two will be working on your own."

Stella exchanged a glance with Maxwell, feeling at once thrilled and terrified at the official confirmation of their first solo case. The pressure was on.

"Why's that?" Maxwell asked.

"The money laundering case that Agent Billings is handling is becoming increasingly complex. The tentacles of the involvement go deep, and they go a long way. So, I said I'd join them on it."

At that, Stella's ears pricked up.

Her rival in the New Haven office, Carrie Potts, was working under Special Agent Billings. Ever since they'd been at the FBI Academy in Quantico together, Carrie had perceived Stella as a threat and had tried her best to jeopardize her career.

Having Roth working closely with her was not an ideal scenario. Carrie was intelligent and sneaky. Stella feared she would do her utmost to poison Roth against her, in subtle ways, while presenting herself as the most capable and sought-after young agent the FBI had ever employed.

Stella already felt under pressure and Roth hadn't yet told them about the case he was handing to them. She wondered what it would be as he opened the file.

"Here's the background. College kid in Putnam by the name of Clint Woods threw a house party while his parents were on a weekend trip out of town. They got back yesterday morning to find the place impressively trashed, and a dead body in the tub in the master bathroom."

"Cause of death?" Maxwell asked.

Given the circumstances, Stella's money was already on a fight. Things had gotten out of hand, alcohol had been a contributing factor, and two of the students had fought. Her mind was already racing ahead to the cause of death. A fist fight could have caused the death, more so if one of the fighters had slipped and fallen. A gunshot was possible, especially since the parents had been away and might have left access to the gun safe.

A stabbing was also in the cards, but it was the cause of death she dreaded the most, thanks to her own experience. She'd never forgotten the utter shock she'd felt waking up next to her fiancé, Vaughn, and finding him in a pool of blood with a knife sticking out of his chest. Some images could never be forgotten. Time didn't heal.

Stella knew she shouldn't assume but couldn't prevent herself from imagining the possibilities as she waited for what Roth would say.

A fight would probably have had witnesses, or people would have overhead it. Both parties might have injuries. Hopefully that would allow them to resolve the case quickly.

Of course, when he spoke, Roth surprised her completely and made Stella wish she hadn't already started visualizing wrong scenarios.

"Victim was a woman. When the crime was called in, they hadn't ID'ed her yet, but I believe they have since done so. They just haven't gotten around to telling us. And the cause of death was strangulation. She had a cable tie slipped around her neck and tightened."

"What?" Stella asked incredulously.

Roth's explanation had veered all the way off-script. Strangled by a cable tie? That wasn't a typical outcome for a drunken college party at all.

Strangulation? She simply couldn't understand it. She saw her own surprise reflected in Maxwell's face as Roth continued calmly.

"Jansen, the assistant investigator from the Putnam Police Department, called me yesterday and asked if we could handle it in tandem with them. I agreed and told him you'll head to the scene immediately after your briefing."

"Why do they want the FBI involved?" Stella asked.

She hoped that this family was not politically connected. She'd had more than enough trouble of that kind in her last murder case.

Luckily, her fears were put to rest by Roth.

"They want us to get involved because Clint Woods is a student at the University of Connecticut, and a lot of his friends and fellow students were at the party. Now, you may or may not know that the University of Connecticut has one of the highest numbers of international students in the wider area, including over a thousand internationals in Applied Mathematics, which is the degree Clint is studying."

Stella didn't know this and was surprised to learn it. Immediately, she could see how this would add to the complexity of the case.

"Forty-nine countries are represented in the university, including many students from China, India, and South Korea. Inevitably, some of them ended up at the party," Roth sighed. "It's a potentially sensitive situation, and there will be international implications if one of them is the killer. Jansen picked up on this immediately and called me. He's been in touch with the university, and they are very anxious that it gets solved fast. You'll be dealing with him, and with Detective Grover, who's in charge."

"I see," Stella said, understanding the importance of their early involvement.

"Head there straight away. It's a developing case and there's new information becoming available by the minute. They'll be able to tell you far more by the time you arrive, I should think. Keep me updated and let me know if there are any problems. If you guys need help, I'll step in, but if you can handle it fast without me, that'll be first prize."

Stella drained her coffee and stood up. She felt ready for the challenge.

She grabbed her purse, and Maxwell signed out the keys for one of the unmarked vehicles. Then they walked out.

"Strangled by a cable tie?" Maxwell said in a soft, disbelieving voice, as they strode down the corridor to the exit.

"It feels surreal. It doesn't make sense. Unless a cable tie was lying around somewhere, just as someone got mad?" Flimsy in the extreme, as theories go, Stella thought. She'd need to start reasoning better than that.

"Could it have been sexual, do you think?" Maxwell asked as they climbed into the unmarked.

"I guess so, but a cable tie? That sounds rather extreme. Sexual strangulation with a silken rope or even a cord from a bathrobe would be more plausible," she said.

Maxwell sighed. "Yeah. My thinking also. We're being thrown in the deep end on something that looks to be far weirder than I thought."

Maxwell's music started up automatically when he hooked his phone up to the car's Bluetooth. Quickly, he turned the sound off. Stella saw him shake his head somberly, as if this was not the time to be airing his eclectic mix of songs. Not when they were on their way to such a serious assignment.

It had started to rain. In the quietness of the car, cold drizzle spattered the windscreen in gusts as they headed out onto the road, and toward the highway that led to Putnam.

As they reached a red light at one of the main intersections, Stella noticed a newspaper billboard that chilled her blood.

"Shock Evidence in Marshall Trafficking Case," it screamed.

She stared at it, feeling sick with worry.

This was her ex's family. In the brief time she'd spent at the Marshalls' Greenwich mansion, she had been the first to uncover the misdoings that the family had been involved in. The police had then investigated and laid charges.

The Marshalls had fought back hard, but from this headline, it seemed like their legal team was getting buried by the mountain of incriminating evidence. If any of the Marshalls were convicted, Stella knew their fury at her would know no bounds. The family already wanted nothing more than to destroy her.

How Stella wished this entire complicated mess would just go away. Instead, it sounded as if it was getting worse.

She turned her head away from the poster, not wanting to read those troubling words again, and stared out of the passenger window as the rain-swept landscape sped by.

She couldn't do anything about the Marshalls, but their vendetta against her meant a constant need for her to perform at her best. She knew that they would quickly get to hear about any weakness, any fault, any mistake she made, and they would use it against her.

The pressure was on to solve her first solo case – fast, thoroughly, and without making any mistakes that might come back to haunt her.

CHAPTER FOUR

An hour and a half later, Stella and Maxwell arrived in Putnam. The address they were looking for was beyond the town center, and seemed to be in a rural area, but Stella was charmed by the town itself as Maxwell detoured down the main street to pick up some bottles of water along the way.

Set alongside what she saw was the Quinebaug River, the town itself was quaint and historic, filled with a mix of antique stores and art galleries, eateries and entertainment venues.

"It used to be an old milling town, I believe," Maxwell said. She guessed the area was new to him as well. Maxwell was a New York resident who'd moved to Connecticut last year after joining the FBI. Clearly as engrossed by the view as she was, he slowed right down to take in the charming theatres and cafés that lined the street.

"Seems like a fun place to spend a day," he said.

The comment was casual, but all the same, Stella couldn't stop herself from filing this possibility away in her mind as a future – date was definitely the wrong word, and she was not going to get ahead of herself by using it. A future outing with Maxwell. Imagine coming here together on a lazy Sunday, strolling around the scenic downtown area, maybe taking in a show or a music performance at one of the theatres, followed by dinner somewhere, overlooking the tree-lined riverbanks.

Reluctantly, she abandoned her dreams as Maxwell drove out of town, accelerating again as he followed the map. There was no time for planning dates or outings. Not when a woman had been murdered in the most horrific way.

"This is the road. Songbird Avenue," Maxwell said.

The Woods family lived out of town, in an upmarket rural area. The stands were enormous, the houses huge, and it took a minute to drive from one gateway to the next. Uneasily, Stella realized it reminded her of the Marshalls' neighborhood.

"Number three," Maxwell said decisively. The lower gate was open. He drove up the winding drive, that led through a woodland of sycamore trees before the mown lawns and imposing frontage of the home came into view.

They parked behind two other small vehicles that Stella guessed belonged to the local police division.

Since the body had been found yesterday, she was relieved that it would have been long since removed. There would be no need to view it on site, although they would have to carefully go through the details of how it had been found. Any information could be crucial.

They got out and hurried toward the front door.

Already, Stella was surprised. The immaculate state of the property ended abruptly at the start of the small formal garden outside the door. The carefully trimmed privet hedges had paper plates and drink cans adhering to their wet leaves. She counted three smashed bottles on the stairs leading to the front door – and beyond, things were worse.

"Check out that plate glass window," Maxwell said in tones of awe, pointing at the massive, star-shaped hole in the lounge window that overlooked a well-kept rose garden.

"Things got way out of control," Stella agreed. The rest of the glass was splattered and smeared. She guessed there had been a food fight. A bottle or a plate, thrown hard, might have caused that breakage.

"It's not going to be easy interviewing witnesses," Maxwell added in worried tones.

"No. I doubt there was a sober person on the property," Stella said.

Like Maxwell, she was starting to feel doubtful about the possibility of solving it quickly.

As they got halfway up the stairs, a sturdy, gray haired detective walked out of the house.

He stood in the front doorway, surveying Stella and Maxwell silently. Stella hesitated, looking up at him. She sensed disapproval radiating from him, though she had no idea why, or what might have caused it.

The detective folded his arms.

Without greeting them, he turned away and shouted an annoyed-sounding question to someone in the house that Stella couldn't see.

"What's going on? I thought you'd canceled this!"

"I explained to you yesterday, sir," an anxious-sounding voice called out in reply.

A moment later, a younger, harassed-looking man ran to the door and the two started speaking in low voices.

Stella turned to Maxwell.

"What's happening?" she whispered. "Do you think there's a problem inside?"

Maxwell shook his head. "I don't know what the issue is. Or who's who. Do you think the older guy's Detective Grover? Let's go and see," he added, clearly getting impatient with being ignored.

Maxwell walked purposefully up the stairs.

"Detective Grover?" he asked.

The detective spoke a few more words to his young colleague before turning in Maxwell's direction. He stared at them unsmilingly.

"And you are?" he enquired.

Stella felt quite sure he knew who they were. There was a subtle insulting tone to his words that made her bristle.

"FBI agents Maxwell and Fall," Maxwell replied. "I believe Special Agent Roth spoke to you just now?"

The detective pressed his lips together, rubbing his stubby fingers over his chin as he considered that statement. Beside him, his subordinate shifted edgily from foot to foot. The young man gave Stella a quick, uneasy glance before turning to his boss as he spoke.

"Seems there's been something of a miscommunication here," the older man said. "Special Agent Roth didn't speak to me. Nobody spoke to me regarding the involvement of any other law enforcement."

He turned and locked his gaze onto the young detective, who looked down.

"I was away this weekend, in New Jersey, at a family funeral. I drove back early this morning and have just arrived at the scene. In my absence, Detective Jansen was handling things. Clearly, he decided that our department was not capable of handling them and called you to do his job for him."

Grover scowled at Jansen, who was looking angry and demoralized at the criticism. Stella couldn't believe it. She'd instantly pegged Grover as a bully. He wanted things done his way or not at all. She didn't know if he had particular issues with the FBI for any reason, or whether this was just his standard response to any interference on his turf.

"It's the right decision for us to be called in," Stella said. She thought Grover was spoiling for a fight. Despite her irritation with him, it would be better to defuse the situation and get things off on a good footing. "I believe there were international students at the house party? So, the FBI needs to be involved."

Now Grover turned and looked at her. Stella bristled at the dismissive set of his mouth.

"You believe wrong, ma'am. Nobody knows as yet who was at this party and who was not. There was a massive amount of underage drinking. As a result, there are a lot of young people who are swearing they were not at the party, or in Putnam, or even in Connecticut at the time."

"I see that," Maxwell tried, but Grover steam-rolled over him.

"And even if they admit to being at the party, they won't have any recall of what they saw. Their versions are completely flawed. We have a bunch of witnesses so unreliable that any good defense lawyer will drill enough holes in the testimony to be sure the case falls apart. And trust me, in these parts, any family whose son is charged with this crime will be able to afford a good defense lawyer."

"I can see that will be a concern," Stella agreed. But Grover raised a warning finger before she could speak further.

"This is not our first rodeo. We've had cases go cold before now, after parties like this. Two others, in the twenty-five years I've been in charge here, where alcohol took front and center stage, and things got out of control. They were never solved. The only outcome was to massively waste police time and resources."

"But –" Stella began, but Grover interrupted her again.

"The chances are very high the same will happen again. But now, thanks to my assistant, we have strangers muscling in, who think they know how to do things better. I can tell you right now, it's going to cause more problems."

He wagged the finger at Stella.

Anger surged inside her. She wished she could grab the finger, twist it hard, and wipe that smug, piggish expression off Grover's round, mustached face.

As well as being a bully, Stella also picked up that Grover was a chauvinist. He wouldn't have wagged his finger at Maxwell like that, and that fact made Stella smolderingly mad.

"Unfortunately, there's nothing you can do about it now, sir," she snapped. "We're officially assigned to the case. It's our responsibility to see it through and we'll do our utmost to solve it, despite the challenges. Now, if you don't mind, we've wasted enough time outside. Can you show us where the protective gear is, and take us to view the scene?"

Even though she spoke with as much authority as she could muster, she couldn't help feeling shaken by Grover's words. Pessimistic as they were, they painted a believable picture. What if they were up against impossible circumstances and the case did grow cold?

Grover lowered his hand. Stella thought he looked briefly furious at her words.

"Take them to the scene," he ordered Jansen. "I need to make a call."

CHAPTER FIVE

Jansen turned and hurried ahead of Stella into the house, clearly as relieved to get away from Grover's domineering presence as she was. In the hallway, he gestured to a box of equipment.

"Please use the foot covers and gloves. We combed the bathroom and bedroom for evidence until late last night, but there wasn't much to be found forensically. Or rather, there was too much to be found everywhere except the scene itself. The bathroom was one of the only places in the house that had been well cleaned before the party and stayed that way. It's easier to access the master bedroom through the glass sliding door, but I guess you'd like to view the house also, so follow me. You'll have to walk carefully and pick your way. We obviously haven't been able to do any cleaning, or moving, while it's still being actively investigated.

"Where is the family staying?" Stella asked.

"They're a family of three. Carolyn and Duncan Woods, and Clint, their twenty-one-year-old son who organized the party. They own a townhouse in a nearby area and have moved there for the next week or so, until this place can be set to rights," Jansen explained.

Jansen spoke fast and, as he moved out of earshot of Grover, Stella picked up the ring of enthusiasm returning to his voice.

"Can you fill us in on the details you have so far?" Maxwell asked, as they quickly slipped on the covers and gloves.

"The victim is Desiree Jardine. She's forty years old, and is recently divorced, with a seventeen-year-old son, Peter. He's still in high school, and stays with his father during term time, so he wasn't at this bash."

Stella felt surprised by this information. Again, the case was twisting away from her expectations. She'd have guessed the victim to be in her early twenties, at a college party.

"So her son wasn't at the party, and she was?"

Jansen nodded. "Yes."

What had she been doing there, Stella wondered? The most likely reason for her presence would be an angry parent storming in to find her child. But he hadn't been invited.

They followed Jansen along the corridor. Stella immediately realized what he meant. The wide passage was like an obstacle course. Dull blue splinters were strewn over the tiles, from a smashed vase that must have been resting on the pedestal near the wall. The framed paintings on the other side of the corridor had also suffered. One was knocked askew, one hanging out of its frame, and one lying crushed and trodden on the ground.

She picked her way carefully through the debris, staring down at a half-eaten burger that already had a few flies buzzing around it.

The sight made her feel briefly nauseous.

"Mrs. Jardine's body was removed yesterday," Jansen said. "The autopsy is being done this morning. The cause of death was undoubtedly strangulation. But they're going to see if they can get more accurate information on the time of death and any other factors."

Stella glanced at the doors they were passing. All were open, and most seemed to lead into spacious guest bedrooms. She glanced into one room where two detectives were working carefully.

The sour smell of vomit assailed her nose immediately. The bed was a mess. The carpet was stained and dirtied. The chic sofa opposite the bed was overturned, and one of the cupboard doors had been ripped right off its hinges.

Quickly, she turned her face away, feeling ill. The aftermath of this party was truly vile. She didn't envy forensics, having to try and extract information from this soiled, stinking environment.

"It's a mess," Jansen said apologetically. "These kids went crazy. I've never seen anything like it before."

Nor had Stella. The level of devastation was shocking.

Again, she remembered Grover's words. Would there be any witnesses who recalled what they saw, and who were credible enough to withstand cross-examination?

"Who found the body?" she asked.

"Some guys at the party. Clint Woods said he was woken by terrified shouts from the direction of the master bedroom at around nine-thirty a.m. He and three friends woke up and rushed there, where they saw the body. By that time, whoever had first shouted, had already fled the scene. Clint's parents arrived home about half an hour later."

Stella could only imagine the level of pandemonium that must have played out. But at least they had four partygoers confirmed as having been on the scene, who would hopefully know others who'd been there.

They had now reached the master suite, and Stella observed that the trail of destruction had gradually lessened along the way. The master suite was undisturbed. It was a splendid room, gorgeously decorated in cream and gold.

Staring at the gigantic bed, the elegant ottoman, the textured cream upholstery on the furniture, Stella couldn't help comparing this formal room to the tiny bedroom in the apartment she rented in downtown New Haven. She was slowly investing in furniture, and the bedroom now contained a double bed, a large bookcase, a wardrobe, and a desk and chair in the corner. That was all she needed. Well, to be accurate, it was also all there was room for, but she was so damned proud of how homey it felt. It was comforting to look at the familiar spines of the novels and psychology books, and convenient to get out of bed and walk one step to the office chair to work on her laptop.

This enormous room didn't feel homey at all.

She wondered what Desiree had been doing in this room. Why had she ended up on this side of the house?

"Here's the bathroom," Jansen explained, leading them in.

She and Maxwell surveyed the large, tiled space, taking in the layout of the room – shower on the left, a large, sunken bathtub on the right, twin basins straight ahead with a toilet to the left beyond them.

"We think the curtain in front of the tub might have been closed. Clint said it was partway open when he arrived there," Jansen said.

"Any prints from the curtain?" Maxwell asked.

Jansen shook his head. "It's textured, waterproofed fabric. We have a few smears. Nothing more."

Maxwell nodded grimly.

"Did it look like she was having a bath?" Stella asked.

"Not at all. She was clothed. And there was no water in the tub," Jansen explained.

"Any signs of a struggle?" Maxwell asked.

Jansen shook his head. "There's no evidence of a fight or struggle taking place. There were some scratches on her neck, at the site of the cable tie, that were most probably self-inflicted by her trying to loosen it, but that will be confirmed in the postmortem."

"Any possibility she was moved after death?" Stella asked.

Jansen nodded. "She could have been, coroner said. It would have had to be very shortly afterward, but someone could have dragged her to that tub to get the evidence out of sight. Her phone was in her jacket pocket, half-underneath her body, and its screen was smashed, which could have happened due to her being moved or dragged."

This seemed to be likely. Why else would she have ended up in an empty bathtub? Most probably, someone had done the deed, and then hidden her body there.

The presence of a phone indicated that theft or robbery had not been a motive. But it meant they would need to request the record of any calls and messages, if the phone itself was so badly damaged.

"Who's the pathologist in this case?" Maxwell asked.

"It's Spencer Glenn. He usually works at New Haven, but he's helping out closer by because there was a major highway accident near here on Saturday night. Her body's at the Farmington county coroner."

Stella knew Glenn and was glad that he would be doing the autopsy.

"You mentioned the guys who found the body ran away? Anyone else do a runner?" she asked.

"Yes, that's the problem. With all the shouting and panic, people woke up and came out of wherever they had been. A lot of people would have left when they saw the extent of the mess or realized what had happened. It would be very unlikely that the killer stuck around."

Unless he lived at the family home, and couldn't leave, Stella revised to herself.

"We have a few names so far. Ten, maybe. But from all accounts, there were well over fifty here on the night," Jansen added.

More than fifty people, drunk, including friends of friends and random arrivals and people they might never know about. Yet again, Stella was reminded of how difficult it would be to pinpoint the killer.

"Jansen!" They all turned, startled by the angry voice shouting from outside the bathroom. It was Grover, on the warpath. "You've spent enough time on the briefing. I need you to complete the paperwork, back at the precinct."

Beside her, Jansen tensed. The easy, conversational atmosphere dissolved. He hurried to the door, with worry now emanating from him.

Grover appeared in the doorway, looking irritable. Stella wondered if the paperwork was a deliberate punishment for Jansen having dared to spend time with the FBI.

"Are you all done in here?" he asked.

"Yes," Maxwell said. "Can we have a look through the case file now?"

Grover's lips tightened again. "No," he snapped. "Not yet. Jansen needs to get it in order first. I won't allow our processes to be interrupted. We have to work methodically."

Stella could see that Maxwell was close to snapping point with this obstructive detective, but he replied calmly, "That's okay. We'll head straight to the coroner's office, and then interview the Woods family. Here's my card. Please message me with their phone numbers and tell them to expect a call from the FBI in the next hour or two."

Having pulled rank in a most satisfactory way, leaving Grover red-faced and fuming, Maxwell headed to the glass side door, and out into the cold, drizzly morning.

They walked quickly across the lawn. Stella was surprised all over again by the size and scale of the grounds. This house was very spacious, and the acreage was immense. No wonder the party had ended up being so wild. There were no neighbors close enough to have called the cops the minute things started getting out of hand.

"Pity we have to deal with that dinosaur," Maxwell commented as they climbed into the unmarked.

"He's terrible. And he resents our being here," she said. "I think he genuinely believes this case won't be solved, and feels Jansen is trying to show him up by calling the FBI. He doesn't want to help us."

Maxwell shook his head. "I guess all we can do is move as fast as possible on it. It's not going to be easy having to outrun the local police, as well as the killer. With any luck, we can get more information from Glenn."

CHAPTER SIX

The county coroner's office had been one of Stella's very first destinations on the first case she'd worked on. As they stepped inside the Farmington coroner's office to sign in, gown up and sanitize, the sights, smells, and sounds of the place brought the old memories flooding back.

That first time, Stella had felt like a stranger, and an unwelcome one, too. She hadn't even been a fully-fledged agent, and she knew that the men resented her presence. The clean, astringent aroma of disinfectant was associated in her mind with the fear and uncertainty she'd felt, and the stomach-clenching nervousness that she would fail and would shame herself at such an important time.

She hadn't failed.

Now, here she was, partnered up with Maxwell and in charge of her very first case, and she felt just as nervous all over again with the step up in responsibility. Not to mention the added pressure of having an unfriendly detective in charge, as well as such a difficult case.

Stella reminded herself that she had succeeded once and could do so again. Grover was being pessimistic, she told herself. He had a preconceived belief that this case would grow cold and didn't intend to direct any effort or resources into finding out who had committed a cold-blooded murder.

Well, she was going to do her best to prove him wrong. A murder victim deserved nothing less. And Grover was jumping to conclusions by visualizing how the court case would play out. A clear motive might well be uncovered once they started digging into the circumstances. Stella didn't know about the other cold cases Grover had mentioned so dismissively, but this one didn't seem like a crime of passion. It looked more preplanned, and preplanning meant a better chance to identify a motive that would lead them to the killer.

Despite the to and fro of activity, a muted silence infused the pathology center. She found herself speaking in a hushed voice, picking up on the atmosphere of the place.

"Autopsy room number five should be down this passage, according to the layout," Stella said.

"Yes. I guess it must be," Maxwell agreed, and his words reminded Stella that her partner, though fiercely intelligent, was also not highly experienced and had only a year's mileage under his belt.

Nerves churned inside her as she walked down the corridor and tapped on the door. Her hands were already damp inside the protective gloves. She knew she could never have done this as a career. It was her least favorite part of an investigation, and she guessed that would never change. Perhaps things would have been different if her first experience of violent death hadn't been waking up next to her fiancé's blood-streaked, blindly staring corpse.

Stella shivered as the door opened, and not just from the frigid temperature at which the aircon was set.

What secrets would this body reveal? Would Glenn have found any important information that could guide them? Stella felt anxious for evidence that would provide a clear starting point.

Masked and gowned, Glenn greeted them with a quirk of his eyebrows.

"Good to see you two again," he said, leading the way to the steel table.

Stella kept her eyes fixed on him, not yet feeling ready to view the corpse.

"Interesting case. The cable tie was an effective strangulation tool, and a horrible one. Obviously, it cut off most of the victim's air and blood supply instantly," Glenn explained.

Stella swallowed, hoping that her discomfort wasn't evident as she imagined this horrific moment playing out.

"She must have lost consciousness very quickly, but you can see she fought it for a few moments, even though it was deeply embedded and unbreakable. The scratch marks on her throat were made by her, clawing at the tie before she passed out."

Stella bit her tongue, hoping that the sudden pain would distract her from the sick dizziness she felt on imagining this woman's struggle.

She had to avenge her. Someone had sadistically caused this horrifying death. That person was walking free, most probably hoping they would never be found. Perhaps they were scared, but there was also the possibility they felt smugly confident that in the chaos of the party, all answers had been lost.

How dare Grover assume this case would never be solved, she thought, feeling furious at his attitude.

Her anger gave her the courage she needed to face the reality of this death. Stella turned to the corpse as Glenn drew the sheet back.

Now that her shock and fear were under control, she could look at the woman and see who she was. Immediately, Stella was surprised. This slim, petite woman with a head of artfully highlighted beach-blond hair, did not look forty. She barely looked thirty. In life, she must have been very attractive. A beautiful, well kept, recently divorced woman.

"She was wearing a lot of jewelry which was still on her person when she was brought in," Glenn said.

Stella nodded. In such a setting, and with this method of death, it confirmed for sure that Desiree had not been killed for what she owned.

That meant she had been killed for who she was. Someone, somewhere, in the drunken, crazy destruction of Saturday night, had acted on a strong motive for murdering this slender, fragile looking woman. Yet again, she felt confused by how anyone could have done such a thing. Murder was so final.

No longer could Desiree speak for herself. It was now up to Stella and Maxwell to piece together her life, her connections, and anything else that might lead them to her killer.

"How much force would this have taken?" Maxwell asked.

"Not so much. She's a petite woman and as you can see, this was tightened from behind. That also rules out the possibility it was a self-inflicted death," Glenn explained calmly. "Cable ties don't release, and they don't break. So someone must have yanked it as tight as possible and then just stepped out of the way."

Stella had to look down for a moment. The image this conjured up was gruesome. This was far from a drunken dare gone wrong. It was deliberate, forceful and intentional.

It must have taken a very cold person to do such a thing. There was a chance Desiree had been the first victim of a psychopathic killer, but in that wild party environment it was more likely that one of the other guests had intended to murder her.

"Do you know the time of death?" she asked.

"Somewhere between two and four a.m." Glenn said.

Stella wondered if the party had been winding down by then, or whether it had still been pumping.

"Do you have the toxicology report yet?" she said, wondering if Desiree had been drinking, and whether this might have made it easier for her killer. If she hadn't been an irate parent arriving to search for her son, the only other option was that she'd been a guest there.

"Not yet. I'll send it to you as soon as I have it," Glenn said.

"Is there anything else unusual you can pick up about this?" she asked.

He shook his head, looking solemn. "I wish there was something else I could tell you that could be helpful."

"Thanks," Stella said.

They headed back through the pathology lab in silence. At the exit, Maxwell peeled off his gloves and checked his phone.

"I've got a message. Not from Grover. From Jansen. He's sent us the phone number and the address for the Woods family. It's in East Windsor. Let's head there now."

Stella glanced behind her, noticing that a black Lexus with tinted windows had been parked in the next-door bay, and had pulled out just a moment after them.

Maxwell slowed at the light, but the other car raced on, turning right just before the light changed. Then it was out of sight.

Probably nothing, Stella told herself. She turned her focus back to the interview ahead. Clint Woods would be their most important witness so far.

He'd held the party. He'd invited the guests, or at least, some of them. And, drunk or sober, he must have been there the whole evening.

Clint could well hold the key to the murderer's identity.

CHAPTER SEVEN

The townhouse where the Woods family was temporarily living was spacious and luxurious, and Stella saw it had a spectacular view of the Connecticut River; although on this overcast morning, the water looked gray and swathed in mist. The bare branches of surrounding trees reached to the cloudy sky.

She knocked on the white-painted door, which was opened instantly by a woman that Stella guessed was Mrs. Woods.

She was tall, slender, with shiny, bobbed brown hair, and carried herself with a graceful bearing, as if she was an ex-model or dancer. From her son's age, Stella guessed she had to be in her forties, although she didn't look it any more than Desiree did.

Worry made her features gaunt and tense.

"Are you the FBI? I'm Carolyn Woods. Please, come this way. I cannot tell you what an utter shock this has been," she said, leading them through the home's spacious and elegantly decorated lounge, out to the glassed patio which had a panoramic view of the river.

A tall, lean man wearing a Hartford Athletics baseball cap was sitting on one of the wicker chairs. He leaped to his feet as soon as they walked in.

"Morning, agents. I won't say it's a good morning. It's not. We're battling to cope with what has happened. I'm Duncan Woods."

"Agents Maxwell and Fall," Maxwell said.

"I wish we hadn't gone away. What a terrible decision. If only we'd known what would happen," Carolyn lamented.

"Did you know that your son was throwing a party?" Maxwell asked.

Carolyn nodded. "Yes. We did know. He held one last year at the same time for about twenty friends. We were home for that one. Everything went smoothly and there were no hitches at all. I don't think we even had a broken glass. It was all over by midnight. So we had no issues with a second one. We didn't think it would be a problem."

"Until it was," her husband added, sounding furious.

Carolyn sighed. "I don't blame my son for this at all. Please, agents, I don't believe it was his fault. I think what happened was out of his control. Out of everyone's control. It was one of those catastrophes that just snowballed, and nobody could predict. I'm just glad he was okay."

"I blame him," Duncan said angrily. "When we arrived home, it was the shock of my life seeing our house trashed. I doubt if insurance will cover any of the damage, and we'd recently spent a lot redoing it. But all of that means nothing compared to the fact that a murder was committed. In our home! In our bathroom!" he sounded outraged.

"Did Clint know you were getting home so soon?" Stella asked.

Carolyn shook her head. "We planned to return on Monday morning. The reason we came home earlier was that we tried to call Clint to check in with him and couldn't get hold of him. We tried twice at about eight a.m., and then decided to drive back, as we were both worried by that time. We both began to suspect the party had gone wrong."

Clint must have thought he'd have an entire day to clean up if his parents were only expected back on Monday. Perhaps that was why things had gotten so wild, Stella guessed.

"The shock I felt when I arrived back to see the place like this!" Carolyn sighed deeply. "Then, the stress of having the police here, and having to move out."

"At least we know Grover," Duncan reassured her.

"Yes. We've known him for many years. We feel in good hands," Carolyn said. Her very different perspective surprised Stella.

"He and his team were very helpful when we had a burglary a couple of years ago," Duncan explained.

"What happened to your son's phone?" Stella asked.

"Nothing. It ran out of battery charge, and he was so drunk he forgot to charge it," Duncan snapped. He scowled, sounding as if he was at the end of his patience.

Stella decided it was time to get onto the sensitive topic of the murder.

"Did you know the victim?" she asked.

"Oh, yes. We knew Desiree quite well," Carolyn said.

"We used to socialize with her and her husband." Now that they were off the topic of his son's misdoings, Duncan surprisingly sounded calmer. "They divorced a few months ago. He moved to Saratoga Springs, and she stayed in their house in Hartford."

"What does her husband do?" Stella asked. "And does Desiree work?"

She asked the second part of the question just as a formality, because she was becoming used to the typical family situation in these circles, where the wife did not work full-time or at all. But Carolyn's answer surprised her.

"Walter owns a big clothing manufacture business," he said. "And Desiree was the marketing director for YD – that's a chain store called Young Designers that specializes in work from up-and-coming young fashion designers. Their offices are based in Hartford, near her home."

That was interesting, Stella thought. So Desiree had a full-time career.

"Could you give me Walter's phone number?" she asked.

"Sure." Carolyn wrote it down and handed it to Stella. She felt relieved to have this information in her possession. Anything that could bypass the obstructive Detective Grover was a win for them.

"I have one more question. Do you know why Desiree was at the party? What reason did she have for being there? Who would have invited a woman from an older age group to a party for twenty-year-olds?" Maxwell asked.

That was an important question. The Woods exchanged a glance.

"I have no idea," Duncan said.

Carolyn shook her head. "I'm sure Clint will know, but we haven't asked him that particular question yet. We hadn't got around to it, with everything else that's happened."

Stella saw her hands were trembling. This entire disaster was clearly an emotionally racking experience for her. Carolyn's part in the interview was over for now, because Stella didn't have any more questions to ask.

"That's fine. I understand," Stella said. "Can we speak to Clint now? We're done with your questioning, so if you could leave, we can interview him here?"

"Sure," Duncan got up, looking relieved "I'll call him."

As soon as he had left, Carolyn jumped to her feet, twisting her fingers nervously as she faced Stella and Maxwell in appeal.

"I don't know how to ask this," she burst out in a frantic semi-whisper. "I'm so frightened that there might be serious implications for Clint, with you being involved, and all." She laced her fingers together, twining them nervously. "I'm so very worried about the impacts upon his future. He's our only boy and he has a bright future, he's had such good grades, and done so well. This has all been a disaster."

Now, Stella realized why Carolyn seemed so unsettled. She was desperate about protecting her son.

"It's not a problem, Mrs. Woods," Stella reassured her. "We just need to understand what happened. Gathering information is the first step."

Carolyn took a deep breath. "Please can I sit in on the interview? I don't want him to say anything in innocence that might incriminate him in any way."

Stella shook her head. She sympathized with Carolyn's anxiety, but with his mother there, Clint was unlikely to speak openly. In fact, Carolyn's determination to protect her son at all costs, made Stella start wondering if there was anything to hide. She needed to focus even more strongly on Clint's movements, and possible motives, on the night.

"We need to interview him on his own," she said firmly.

Carolyn gave a frustrated sigh. Reluctantly, she headed back into the house as Clint walked out onto the deck.

At first glance, Stella could see that Clint did have a bright future and she could understand his mother's concern. He was tall, fit, with tawny brown hair, bright blue eyes, and a strong, chiseled face.

She guessed he would, in other circumstances, have a flashing smile, but the events of the past twenty-four hours had clearly dented his morale. His head was lowered. He glanced nervously at the agents.

"Morning, ma'am. Morning, sir," he mumbled before standing in the center of the wooden floor, clasping his fingers and twining them together – a habit Stella guessed he had picked up from his mother.

"Morning, Clint. Please sit," she invited him.

He backed to the nearest chair and perched uneasily on it.

"We're not here to make trouble for you," Stella reassured him, even though she could see Clint didn't believe her words. "We're here to catch a killer and to get as much information as we can on what happened. So, can you tell me how the party escalated into such a big event? What happened?"

She waited.

After a while, Clint frowned, as if he was wondering the same. "It was supposed to be just me and my close friends," he said. "But then one friend asked if he could bring his younger brother, and another asked if he could bring a few girls along, and I think they also invited others, and before I knew it, it seemed like it was going to be the bash of the year. We thought – well, we thought it would be fun. I called the caterers and got extra food arranged, and went and got a few more cases of beer, and also some tequila. But then, it got out of control. So many guys pulled in. I tried to keep a lid on things, but I was also drunk."

Stella nodded. Like everyone at the party, he was a suspect until cleared, but she heard only truth in his voice and guessed that he had tried his hardest to contain the situation until it exploded.

"In the end I just kept reminding people my parents' bedroom was off limits and I partied along with everyone else," Clint confessed.

Stella remembered that the master bedroom had been undamaged. Partying had not taken place there. Why, then, had Desiree ended up there, dead?

"Did you invite Desiree?" Stella asked.

Clint shook his head. "Like I said, a lot of people showed up who hadn't been invited," he said.

"Are you sure? With her being a friend of your family?" Stella asked.

Clint shrugged. "I invited my university friends and a few others. Not her. I didn't see who she arrived with. I don't know how she heard about it, but I thought it was pretty cool she was there. She's fun. I've seen her at parties before, recently. She likes to hang with the guys."

He was sticking to his story, but Stella also had the impression he wasn't telling everything he knew. A forty-year-old who routinely attended college parties sounded strange. It was starting to paint a very different picture of Desiree. Had the divorce caused her to behave this way, she wondered.

"Did you socialize with her at any of the previous parties?" Stella asked.

"No. We said hi when we saw each other, but that was about it."

"What about her ex-husband? Did you see him at your party? Any other of her family turn up?"

"It was just her. At my party, and also the past few times I saw her," Clint confirmed.

"What else do you remember about her on the night of your party? Was she spending time with anyone in particular? Did she speak to you at all?"

Clint sighed. "I don't remember much. It was a blur. I mean, I knew things were getting crazy, but I actually didn't realize how crazy. We had a tequila drinking competition, and I got sick, and then I partied again. Some guys were doing these out-of-control food fights and things were getting smashed. I tried to stop them, but I was feeling really tired by then. I went and locked myself in my bedroom. I kind of hoped that I'd wake up and all the mess I remembered would be a dream."

Stella considered this statement. It seemed like a valid account, given the circumstances. But locking himself in his bedroom meant his movements were unaccounted for during part of the night. That might be significant.

"When did you wake up?" Maxwell asked, clearly thinking along the same lines.

"When some people started yelling. I woke up with a big fright. I was so confused." Clint ran a hand through his hair. "At first I thought there was a fire, that they had set the place on fire somehow. That was one of the things I was worried about that night, with everything being so wild. But then I saw it was morning. So I rushed out. I met a couple of friends in the corridor, and we figured out that the noise had been coming from my folks' room. so we headed there. By that time. I was already freaking out that something bad had happened. We got into the room and checked the bathroom and we saw – we saw – her."

His voice started wobbling. He buried his head in his hands.

"I don't know how to forget that sight. I don't think I ever will. It's like a nightmare. I can't get to sleep now without seeing it." Raising his head, he stared at them in appeal.

"Does it ever get better?" he asked miserably.

His response was totally authentic. This murder had shocked Clint to his core. This visceral horror was not the response she expected from somebody who was the perpetrator. Nothing was certain, but most probably his horrified reaction cleared him as the killer. She still wanted to find out if he'd been alone with Desiree during the evening, and how it had played out. Since he'd denied spending time with her, she'd have to check if anyone else had noticed them together.

"Your folks should send you for counseling," she said sympathetically. "You need to talk this through with somebody."

"I – yeah. I guess so. I don't think they want to do anything for me right now," he said. "Especially Dad. Dad's furious."

"Perhaps in a few days," Stella suggested. "For now, though, I need you to make a list of everyone you remember, and recognize, from having been at that party."

Clint stared at her, wide-eyed at this fresh bombshell.

"Do I have to?" he pleaded.

Maxwell nodded.

"But –with so many underage guys, I feel like I'm going to get them into serious trouble. I don't want anyone getting a criminal record for underage drinking because I ratted them out. I didn't mean for this to happen!"

"We are not investigating who was underage drinking. That is not our mandate," Stella emphasized. "Our mandate is to catch the killer. As such, we need your full cooperation." She stared at him sternly.

"Okay. Okay. I'll write the list," Clint agreed in a small voice. "But please, don't get the guys in trouble. I don't want things to get any worse," he pleaded.

Clint promised to send through the list in the next hour. With no more questions to ask, Stella and Maxwell left the luxuriously equipped townhouse.

Now they knew about the reasons for the party, and some of the fragments of what had played out that evening. But Stella wanted to learn more about the past.

The motive for the crime most probably stretched back further than the night of the party itself. Given the recent divorce, and Desiree's subsequent behavior, Stella was particularly curious about the couple's history and the reasons for the split-up.

As they walked out, she dialed the number for Walter Jardine, hoping they could speak to him immediately. The divorce could have been acrimonious. And there could have been issues with alimony. As Stella knew, fights over money could trigger the most nefarious crimes – up to and including murder. Clint hadn't noticed Desiree's ex-husband at the party, but Clint had said he'd locked himself in his bedroom for the latter part of the evening.

Stella wanted to find out more about this divorce, and whether Walter had a motive for murdering his wife.

Walter answered almost immediately, sounding stressed, and as if he was driving.

"I'm not in Saratoga Springs at the moment," he told Stella. "I'm on my way to Desiree's home in Hartford, to pack up her things. I'll be arriving there in fifteen minutes."

This haste to go through his ex-wife's possessions triggered Stella's suspicions. Why was Walter so urgently heading to the house?

"We'll meet you there as soon as possible," she said.

CHAPTER EIGHT

Half an hour later, Stella pulled up outside Desiree's home in Hartford.

She felt impatient to know why Walter was in such a rush, and wished she'd been able to get to Hartford faster.

Since they were under pressure of time, and the YD offices were a block away from her home, she'd dropped Maxwell there to interview Desiree's co-workers. Stella would be going solo on this interview, and as she climbed out of the car, she reminded herself to be alert for any signs that Walter was trying to lie.

The home was located on a quiet, suburban street. It was a serene and beautiful area. The gracious homes on the street had sweeping front lawns, and a backdrop of tall trees and homestead elms. Stella guessed that the homes backed onto a park or nature preserve. Rain was threatening again, and the lowering, gray sky made the scene appear somber and muted.

A brand-new white Range Rover stood in the driveway with its doors open. The home's front door was also open.

Walter Jardine was most definitely not wasting any time moving things out. At least she could now see what he was doing, and what items were getting so hastily packed into that big, shiny car.

Stella hurried up to the front door, and as she reached it, she saw the reason for the rush.

A teenager with spiky, sandy-blond hair was hurrying toward the front door. He looked distressed and gripped a cat carrier carefully in his arms.

"Good afternoon," he stammered out.

Stella's suspicion ebbed, and in its place, she felt a rush of sympathy for him. He hadn't been at the party, or in the area. He was not a suspect and was an innocent victim in the tragedy.

"Are you Peter Jardine?" she asked, to clarify.

"Yes, I am," he said miserably.

"I'm so sorry about what's happened. You must be so shocked," Stella sympathized.

"I – yes, I am. I don't think it's sunk in yet," he admitted. "When Dad and I heard, we came straight here. She has lots of animals and we were very worried about them. We're moving them to Dad's home now."

Stella looked past him, to see an older man appear from around the corner. He led two corgis on leashes and held another cat carrier in his other hand.

"Walter Jardine," he said somberly. He no longer sounded stressed. He spoke in a calm, measured tone that seemed to fit his personality.

Stella was surprised by how much older than Desiree he appeared. Walter must be well into his fifties, she thought. His age was not artfully concealed, but starkly visible in his graying hair, his slight paunch, and the lines on his face which she guessed looked harsher than usual, thanks to the stress of what had happened.

"Agent Fall," she said. "I'm so sorry about this. It must be such a shock for you."

Even if Walter was his ex-wife's killer, it would be wrong and inhumane not to offer sympathy at such a time, and in the presence of their son.

"It's unbelievable. Unreal," Walter agreed. He placed the cat carrier on the ground and handed the dog leashes to his son.

"Will you put Gucci and Prada in the car? Make sure you fasten the leashes so that they can't jump out."

Gucci and Prada. The dogs' names definitely indicated their late owner's love for fashion, Stella thought sadly.

The instructions to his son were clearly a subtle message for him to leave the house. As soon as he had walked out, Walter indicated a door on the right.

"Perhaps we can move into the lounge? I would rather not have my son overhear the conversation. He's very traumatized."

"Sure," Stella said.

"I don't know what I can tell you. Desiree and I divorced at the end of July. I relocated to be closer to my business. We agreed Peter would spend term time with me and vacation time with his mother," he added somberly.

Stella was surprised by what a different person he was than she'd expected. Her impressions so far of Desiree had been that she was a fun-loving woman. That was definitely the picture Stella had. This man was far more serious. He seemed a different generation from her, she thought, confused. She could see why they might have split up and felt the divorce might have been a long time coming.

"What was the reason?" she asked, to clarify her suspicions.

"She wanted more out of life. I was working very hard and preferred a quieter lifestyle. Especially as Peter grew older, and became less dependent on us, she wanted to have fun. To party, to travel. I guess I'd never been that person and my work commitments are still very intense. So we divorced, but remained on friendly terms. When she was away, which was often, either Peter or I would come and house-sit to make sure the animals were okay."

"Did you know if anything unusual was happening in her life? Anything worrying her? Any recent fights or conflict?" Stella asked.

Walter thought carefully about the question.

"No. We didn't have the kind of relationship after the divorce where we would confide in each other about personal issues. We kept that out of the picture. Our conversations were mainly about Peter, his schedule, and if any of the cats or dogs needed any special care. I made a special effort not to ask her if she was seeing anyone else. I felt that if she wanted me to know, if it was serious, she would tell me. And to be honest with you, I didn't really want to know if she was."

"How did you feel about the divorce?" That comment indicated he had divorced reluctantly, Stella thought.

Walter made a face. "I was unhappy about it, but there was nothing I could do. She cited irreconcilable differences, and I could see that they did exist. But in a way I hoped that she'd be able to enjoy her freedom for a while and would then decide to settle down and we could start afresh. I'd always had that hope. That perhaps it wasn't going to be forever, and that we could get back together one day. She was a fun, lovely person. Whenever she was around, she made the day seem brighter," he added sadly.

"Did Peter ever tell you about anyone else in her life?" Stella asked.

"No. He always said that Mom was alone when he visited her. She did activities with him. They were forever going out to movies, restaurants, going on day trips. But it was just the two of them."

"Were you aware she was attending college parties from time to time?" Stella asked.

Walter shrugged. "Like I said, we didn't speak about our social lives. But Desiree worked in the fashion industry, and attended a lot of events with young people, models, designers. She always got on well with them."

"What did the divorce mean for you financially?" Stella asked. Even though Walter didn't sound like he had any reason to kill his wife, she wanted to be sure and explore every possible motive.

"Nothing, really. Her job was very well paying, and she had inherited some family money from her father's side. We agreed on no maintenance payments but that I should continue paying for Peter's high school and college education which I was happy to do."

"Did you initially offer to pay maintenance? Did she request it? How did this agreement work out?" Stella asked. After all, with a murder conviction at stake, anyone could lie. Even serious-seeming, responsible people.

"I offered originally, but she refused and said there was really no need. It made sense, as she had always worked full-time in a career she loved, and in any case Peter would be spending more time with me. Which we were both comfortable with," he said thoughtfully.

"Where were you on the night of the party?" Stella asked.

"I was home, in Saratoga Springs. Peter was with me. He had a couple of friends over for the night."

Stella nodded. There was no bad blood between them. There were no money issues. Walter had been keen to resume the relationship at some future stage and had spent the evening at home with his son. Stella couldn't discern any motive whatsoever and decided there was no need for further questioning.

"Thank you for your time," she said.

She walked out of the lounge. Looking outside, she saw the cat carriers were safely stowed in the Range Rover's trunk, and Stella could hear excited barking coming from the back seat. She was glad all the animals would be safely cared for. But, in terms of information, the interview had not been rewarding.

She hoped that Maxwell would have had better insights.

There he was. His questioning could not have taken long, because he was already heading to the unmarked at a swift walk, ducking his head to avoid the gusty rain that had started to fall.

Stella climbed into the car to wait for him.

A moment later, Maxwell jumped in. He shook water off his dark hair. She smelled the fresh tang of rain, and the damp wool of his suit jacket.

"Should've taken an umbrella," he said ruefully.

"What did you learn?" she asked.

"Her colleagues are pretty much in chaos. Heartbroken. The managing director has just flown in from Buffalo. They can't believe it, can't understand it, had no idea who could have done it. Their theory is a random psycho."

Stella shook her head. "We can't rule that out, I guess."

"She had no conflict with co-workers. They said she was a very hard worker. When I asked, they said she socialized a lot, but never drank at weekday work functions, and would have one glass of wine if there was a weekend function."

"That's useful to know," Stella said. So, Desiree hadn't blurred the boundaries between work and social life.

"They didn't discuss each other's private lives much. No real reason. There weren't a lot of people in the Hartford office full-time, which I think contributed to that. It was a satellite office, mainly used for marketing and some admin. She flew to Buffalo for meetings every week or two. They were aware she'd had an amicable divorce a while ago," Maxwell glanced at Stella.

She nodded. "That confirms what Walter said. The divorce was amicable, there were no conflicts over alimony, and she loved her job and was good at it."

Maxwell sighed. "Where are the problems, Fall? What aren't we seeing? Why was this woman, with a seemingly perfect life, murdered in such a way?"

Stella shook her head. She felt his frustration. If only there were answers, or at least a lead that would help them in the right direction.

But Desiree hadn't had a normal life, especially after the divorce. Despite what her husband had said, she'd been partying with university students half her age on a regular basis. This hadn't been related to her work. It was something different from the usual and it provided a glimpse that everything was not as it should be.

Maxwell's phone beeped. He glanced down and his annoyed expression relaxed.

"Hopefully this might open some doors. You've probably also received it. It's the list of Clint's friends."

"Let's get onto it right now," Stella said, feeling motivated all over again. She scrutinized the list of names.

Her first impression was that Clint had done a good job. It was a long list, and he'd included many of the phone numbers and where he couldn't, he'd added details such as the area they lived, and the university and class they attended.

"There are a lot of names here," Maxwell said. "Twenty or more."

"I guess we should split up then," Stella suggested.

"We're going to have to. Interviewing all these guys is going to take time, unless we get lucky with the first one that we speak to," Maxwell said.

"You start from the bottom; I'll take the top?" she suggested.

"Sounds good," Maxwell agreed. "Let's drive back to New Haven so you can get a car, and then see where we are in a couple of hours."

Out of the names on this carefully compiled list of people who had been at the party, someone must have seen or heard something that could be critical to the case. If she could ask the right questions, they might get closer to the answers they needed.

CHAPTER NINE

The first name on Stella's list, right at the top, belonged to Ollie Small, who lived in a townhouse in Ridgewood. She was now standing outside this home, under the sheltered porch, in the pouring afternoon rain.

Being first on the list, Stella wondered if Ollie was a good friend of Clint's. Unless he'd decided to hide his friends near the bottom of the list to protect them, she revised.

She knocked, and a minute later, the door was opened by a harassed-looking, forty-something year old woman who Stella guessed must be Ollie's mother.

"Are you Mrs. Small? I'm Stella Fall from the FBI," she said.

The woman paled. "You're from where?" she repeated in a soft voice.

"From the FBI, investigating the murder," Stella elaborated.

The stress on Mrs. Small's face instantly morphed to fury.

"I do not believe this! Do not believe it!" she exclaimed. "Our lives have turned into a complete nightmare as a result of this damned party! My son might get a criminal record for underage drinking, and now he's a murder suspect!"

She spread her arms wide in frustrated appeal.

"I understand, ma'am," Stella sympathized. "This is a very difficult situation."

"I am so angry with him," Mrs. Small confided through gritted teeth. "He's only twenty. He lied to us, and said he was going to go gaming with a friend and would sleep there overnight. Next thing, he's calling us in the morning sounding absolutely wretched. Saying something terrible has happened and we must come and fetch him immediately."

Stella nodded in agreement.

Mrs. Small sighed. "Now our whole community knows what happened and that he was there. It's going to be talked about for months. Can I sit in when you speak to him?"

It seemed that all the parents were worried about their wayward sons making a bad situation worse. Reluctantly, Stella declined this request.

"I need to speak to him alone. The interview will be confidential unless he gives us information that is directly relevant to the murder."

"Okay. Okay." It seemed Mrs. Small was gathering her courage together. "Let me call him and get his younger brother and sister out of the way. Do you want to wait in the family room?"

She gestured to a doorway straight ahead.

Stella walked through and found herself in a room that surprised her with its homeliness. The comfortable looking couches were scuffed. The only alternative seating was two worn bean bags. A bookshelf was untidily piled with books. A pink-outfitted Barbie doll perched atop a palomino horse clued Stella that there was a fair-sized age gap between Ollie and his younger sister.

As she sat down on one of the couches, an apprehensive-looking young man entered the room.

"Hi – good morning. Um, I mean, good afternoon," he said, glancing at the clock on the wall, while looking awkward and scared.

"Hi, Ollie. I'm Stella Fall. Sit down, please," Stella invited.

"I'm so sorry. My mom said this is going to mean big trouble." Ollie sat down. He was a gangly man, all long limbs and elbows. Just like Clint, he, too, looked rather pale, as if the monster hangover might still be lingering.

"This is a confidential interview. We're looking for background on the murder," Stella reassured him.

He didn't seem convinced by her words but took a deep breath as if preparing himself for the ordeal ahead.

"How did you hear about the party?" Stella asked.

"My friend Cheung heard about it. We're doing the same applied math degree, so we party together a lot. Cheung's friends, Him-Chan and Iseul, had been invited by Clint, but they said that it was an open party and everyone could come along. We decided we'd meet up there as a group."

All three of those names appeared on Stella's list. She listened carefully as Ollie continued.

"I know Clint slightly from university. So it wasn't like he was a total stranger, so we decided hey, why not. And I did unfortunately tell my folks something different. I didn't want them to worry. I didn't know things would go so bad. I regret having done that," he told Stella earnestly.

"Did you know many of the people there?" she asked.

"Apart from the three I met up with, none of them were my close friends. Clint and I are in different years. He's a year ahead of me so I don't really know who he hangs out with."

"Did you see Desiree Jardine, the murder victim, at all?"

"Yes, I saw her arrive. We all noticed her because she was really good looking. I mean, some of the people around here have been saying she was forty, but she didn't look it."

"She was forty," Stella confirmed, and Ollie looked surprised.

"Anyway, she was with a couple of guys who I also didn't know. They got there soon after we did. There was a group of girls behind them, and I remember thinking maybe she was part of that group and got talking to the guys on the way in."

"Can you describe the guys she was with?" Stella asked.

Ollie shook his head. "I wasn't really looking at them. I was looking at her."

"Did you speak to her at all?"

"No. No, I didn't. We just stayed in the background and ended up drinking way too much. We watched her. She and some of the other girls were acting really wild. She was flirting with quite a few of the guys. Including Clint."

Stella noted that comment with interest. Clint hadn't mentioned it. Now, a different version was coming out. She wondered how Clint had felt about that flirtation.

"I mean, it looked like she was having a ball. She didn't seem to be afraid or in danger," Ollie frowned thoughtfully, as if expecting that someone who was about to be murdered should surely have been scared.

"Did you speak to Clint at all?"

"We spoke to him at one stage when we were getting more tequila. He told us we must please not go into his parents' room and that we mustn't break things. I thought he looked stressed, like this whole party had gotten out of his control. Which it had, of course. After that, people were smashing things and going crazy. There was a big fight by the door as well. It sounded like someone was getting thrown out."

"Did you see the fight, or know who was involved?" Stella asked. It was the first she'd heard of a fight and wondered if it was significant.

"No. I didn't see anything. I think that was at about one-thirty in the morning, because after that happened, the three guys I was with decided to leave. Cheung said he was worried the party was getting out of hand and he didn't want to get into trouble. They decided to Uber back to the university. They asked if I wanted to share the ride and go back via my house, but I wasn't ready to leave, and said I'd go later. They tried to persuade me to change my mind. Now, I wish I had listened to them. They called their ride and left, and I went back inside. I planned to party some more, but when they had gone, I realized how drunk I was. I felt so tired, I went to sleep behind one of the couches."

Ollie looked briefly thoughtful. Stella wondered if he was recalling something.

"Any other details you remember?" she probed.

He hesitated, and then made a face. "I heard a few people coming and going, but I don't remember much more until suddenly everyone started shouting in the morning."

"Are you sure?" Stella asked.

"Yes. I'm sure," Ollie said, more confidently now. But Stella wasn't convinced. She thought he'd been about to tell her something and then decided against it.

"Remember, even if it seems unimportant, we need to know the details," she pushed.

Ollie made a rueful face. "If I remember, I'll tell you."

"You will not get in trouble for telling us, even if it's not totally accurate info," she encouraged, planting the seed that might encourage him to talk.

"I'll keep that in mind," he said hesitantly.

"Were you behind one of the couches in the lounge?" Stella asked, wanting to get a picture of where he had been.

"No. There's a family room down the passage, I think it was opposite one of the bedrooms. I wanted to get away from the smashing and shouting. I was feeling cold by then and that room was warm. So I just lay down out of the way."

"Thank you," Stella said.

She waited a while, but it was clear that Ollie wasn't ready to talk. Or perhaps it really had been an irrelevant memory that he didn't want to tell her about, like throwing up all over the carpet.

"I appreciate your honesty," she said eventually, and handed him a card. "Please call me if you remember anything else at all."

She couldn't think of anything else to ask. Teasing the bigger picture from the confused accounts of fearful and reluctant witnesses was going to be a delicate task, especially with so many complex reasons for why people didn't want to tell everything they knew. Eventually, the glimpses might start to piece together.

Stella got up and walked to the front door. As she headed to the car, she heard a frantic shout from behind her.

Turning, shielding her eyes against the spattering rain, she saw Ollie burst out of the front door and sprint toward her.

"I'm sorry, ma'am. Sorry to bother you again but there's something else," he said, sounding breathless.

"What else?" Stella asked. Then, realizing how wet they were both getting, she added, "Let's talk in the car."

They hurried to the car. Stella climbed in the driver's side and Ollie scrambled into the passenger seat.

"It's something strange," Ollie explained, brushing water away from his face. "I don't know if it was real or not. I was going to tell you and then thought no, it would be wasting your time. But then I thought it might be helpful, and I should explain."

"I'm glad you decided to," Stella said. At this stage, any additional fragment of information might help. "Can you describe what happened?"

"When I was behind the couch, there was a moment when I woke up. The whole room was spinning, and I felt really ill. I thought I was going to have to go and throw up in one of the bathrooms." He glanced at her, looking embarrassed.

"Go on," Stella said.

"There was no way I wanted to throw up in that lounge. It was too fancy. So anyway, I tried to force myself awake enough that I could move. But at the same time, I was so tired I didn't know if I was dreaming or not. And I think I heard this voice say, 'We must talk.' But it might have been a dream."

"Who said the words?" Stella asked, wondering why Ollie had thought this was so important.

Ollie made a face. "I'm really not sure. I can't even say what the voice sounded like, but I remember it because the next thing, from the couch, I heard, 'Oh, hey! Yes, we must!' really loudly."

"And that was someone different?"

"I thought the second person was Desiree. She has this very high, loud voice. But it could have just been a dream."

“If you had to guess, would you say it was real or not?” Stella asked.

“I would say her voice was, definitely. I don’t know about the rest of it. I can’t be sure if I even remembered it right.”

“Do you know what time it was?”

“No idea. But knowing she was there made me decide not to get up. I mean, she’s this really hot woman? And I’m going to crawl out from behind the couch and go throw up somewhere? Whether it was a dream or not, it sobered me up, enough that the room stopped spinning so badly and I went back to sleep.”

“That could be useful. If you remember anything else, please call me. Any time,” Stella said.

“I will,” he said, looking relieved to have this confession off his chest.

Ollie climbed out of the car and rushed back to the house, leaving Stella wondering how accurate his recall was, and what the significance of that short conversation might be.

Then she glanced behind her and noticed a black Lexus parked nearby.

It was the sleek, shiny, brand-new shape of it that got alarm bells ringing in Stella’s mind. She was certain it was the same car that she’d seen outside the pathologist’s office.

Was it really the same or was she just being paranoid? There had been an XD in the number plate, she remembered; that was all she’d noticed when it had pulled out so suddenly behind her.

There was an XD in this plate, she saw, with a clench of her stomach.

Any other identifying features? Staring anxiously through the rain-spattered glass, she wished she could see beyond those darkly tinted windows.

The hood had a small dent on the right-hand side. That was a useful feature to remember.

As she stared at the car, it pulled smoothly away.

Coincidence? Or had the driver seen her looking?

Stella wondered what this was about. She wished she had more experience to cope with this added complication in an already difficult case. If she saw the driver again, she decided she would face her fears and confront him – or her. She’d find out what their business was, and why they were tailing her.

As she started the car, her phone rang. It was Maxwell calling. She answered eagerly, hoping this meant he'd had a breakthrough with one of his interviews.

CHAPTER TEN

Maxwell headed up the wide, tiled stairs to the home's front porch. There, his first interviewee was already waiting, lounging against the frame of the open front door while she stared down, combing her pink-nailed fingers through the blond tips of her ponytail.

She looked up when she saw him. Her face brightened briefly as her gaze flicked over him. Maxwell guessed that would be because he was relatively tall, fit, and dark haired.

Hopefully, this might give him some credibility points with the young woman that he sensed immediately was snobbish, image-conscious, and on the defensive after having been at a party where a murder occurred.

Her copybook was blotted and now she was angry at the world, and law enforcement in particular.

"Are you Jessica Duarte?" he asked.

With a sigh, she confirmed. "Yeah. You're the FBI agent, right?"

"Agent Maxwell. Can we talk inside?"

Another deep sigh from the entitled Jessica conveyed the extreme inconvenience of having to walk an extra few yards. Flipping her ponytail back over her shoulder, she led the way into the house.

This was one of the most extravagant homes Maxwell had ever stepped inside. It was immaculate. Above the burnished hall table was a huge, garish oil painting. Marble sculptures graced the corners of the hall.

As Jessica flounced into the lounge, which could easily have sat thirty on the magnificent long couches, ottomans, and designer chairs, Maxwell acknowledged that he'd come a long way since he'd first been exposed to the levels of wealth that so many in this society possessed.

He'd started out feeling resentful, and even angry, toward the ultra-wealthy, with their enormous fortunes and their easy lives. He hadn't been able to bridge the disconnection between their background and his own – which had been tough and underprivileged. He remembered the immense sacrifices his mother had made to put her three kids through school. Maxwell remembered how she'd come home in the early hours after finishing her second job, and the terrible feeling of helplessness as he heard his always positive and cheerful mother sobbing as she climbed into bed. That was from what she later confessed to him was sheer exhaustion.

All three of her kids had gotten scholarships to university. They'd inherited her fierce determination, motivated by her burning desire that her children should have a better and easier life than she had endured.

It had taken Maxwell a while to understand that wealth and happiness were two different, and not always synonymous, things. He'd managed to achieve a fair degree of wealth in his IT career before joining the FBI, but while doing so, he'd learned that personal happiness was something different. It was up to him, each day, to create it, nurture it, or to destroy it.

Now, he often felt pity, rather than anger, especially for the children of ultra-wealthy families. Their lives were often complex and over-controlled, far from carefree, so different from what his had been. They had so few options. At least he'd been able to make his own decisions about what his future would be.

Given the choice today, he wouldn't have switched lives.

As a result of his mindset, he was able to give Jessica a brief and genuinely sympathetic smile as he sat down on the ten-seater couch.

"Must have been a tough time for you over this past day," he said to Jessica.

He was glad to see her demeanor unfroze slightly.

"You have no idea," she confided in him, rolling her eyes. "I've been through hell. It's like, everyone who doesn't know me well, thinks I had something to do with it? I so didn't. And I was actually invited by Clint. I wasn't one of the fifty gatecrashers that trashed the place."

"It sure was trashed," Maxwell agreed. "But it must be difficult for you to deal with unfair opinions."

As he sympathized with her, he found himself thinking all over again of Stella Fall.

She had such an incredible way about her with people. It was uncanny the way she could get into their minds – and under their skin, too, when she needed to. He'd started out being resentful of her and ready to find fault with everything she did, but that gentle, probing interview technique of hers had quickly impressed him.

He'd learned so much from her. But there was still so much left to learn. She didn't reveal her own personal issues. She preferred it when others talked.

The way she looked at you with those intense blue eyes, with wisdom and a touch of humor lurking behind that piercing gaze…

Hurriedly, Maxwell returned his thoughts to the interview at hand. He'd meant to channel Fall's best qualities and had ended up daydreaming about her. He needed to focus now. He couldn't afford to lose a moment's attention during this questioning.

"Did you know Desiree Jardine, the murder victim, at all?"

Jessica gazed at him suspiciously.

"Why are you asking me this? What have you heard about her?"

Maxwell decided to answer honestly, hoping it would encourage a like-for-like response.

"Not a lot. We've only been on this case a few hours. So I'm keen to get your personal impressions. Of her behavior on Saturday night, as well as any general thoughts you have."

Jessica considered the question, resting her perfect chin on her thumb.

"I saw her at a few parties recently. And I thought her behavior was pretty disgusting. I mean, seriously? A forty-year-old, hanging with twenty-year-olds? Was she trying to relive her youth or what?"

Jessica's tones resounded with contempt. Watching her, Maxwell had the strong feeling she had a personal problem with Desiree.

"Have you noticed this behavior for a while now?" he asked.

"Yes. Probably a few months. Someone told me she was divorced a while ago. I guess that would be the reason for it. Maybe because her husband didn't want her, she decided to get with any guy who'd let her close enough."

Contempt now dripped from her words.

"Get with?" Maxwell saw where this was going, but pretended to be confused, hoping that Jessica would provide more facts. This was the first hard evidence they'd had of Desiree's reason for being at the party, and it could be vitally important.

"Get with. As in, the trash bag used to sleep around. She was like, a cougar. A sad, nympho cougar. I know she's dead and I shouldn't say such things, but that behavior was out of line." Jessica's eyes flashed and her fists bunched. She was genuinely furious.

"So you think it was, like, a new habit for her?" Maxwell made sure to sound incredulous, so that Jessica would get the reaction she was hoping for. With any luck, this would spur her on to tell more.

"I know it was. I was unlucky enough to be personally affected by that disgusting habit of hers."

"How do you mean?" Maxwell asked.

"There was this guy," Jessica sighed. "This is confidential, right?"

"Yes, it is," Maxwell promised, leaning forward with his elbows on his knees. He was aiming for a nonthreatening, guy-next-door approach.

"Anyway, he is – was – really nice. And into me, I thought. We had a nice, flirty vibe going. He was very cool. On the football team. Handsome. And he threw a party, back in September, and invited me. So I was very excited."

"I guess it didn't go down like you hoped?" Maxwell questioned, with genuine sympathy.

"Desiree was there. And she took one look at him and just...," Jessica spread her hands, looking angry and frustrated. "She just took over. She flirted with him, and she basically seduced him. The last I saw, they went upstairs together."

"Was it serious for either of them? Or just fun for her?" Maxwell asked.

"How should I know?" Jessica retaliated. "I haven't spoken to Mark since then, and the vibe between us disappeared, just like that. But I guess it was just fun, because a friend of mine told me he was bragging to his friends about it afterwards."

Now she wrapped her arms miserably around herself, hugging herself as if she was cold.

Maxwell's attention sharpened. This behavior gave Jessica a possible motive for the murder. Hurt and angry, had she acted recklessly? He made a mental note to check what time she'd left, and what her movements were in the latter part of the night.

Even if Jessica wasn't the killer, this behavior could definitely have been a contributing factor to Desiree's murder. Desiree might have thought she'd just been having fun but getting briefly involved with numerous younger guys was like playing with fire. Emotions, at that age, were powerful things.

"So she did this with a few different guys?" Maxwell asked, to make sure he had the right idea of what was going on. "It wasn't just a random incident?"

Jessica shook her head adamantly. "It definitely was not a once-off. In my opinion, that's why she went to those parties. Because she liked to sleep with younger guys, and she didn't care whose lives got messed up along the way. It's not appropriate. And it's very destructive."

She lifted her chin and gazed at him with the lofty certainty of all her probably twenty-two years.

"I can see that was damaging behavior," he agreed. "Do you know if she went with anyone in particular on the night of Clint's party?"

Maxwell held his breath as he waited for Jessica to answer. A 'yes' might solve the case, then and there.

"No," she said to his disappointment.

"You sure?" he tried.

"Actually, I was really angry when I saw her there."

Maxwell nodded, noting this fact as Jessica continued.

"I tried to avoid her which was difficult because she liked to be the center of attention. Eventually, my girlfriend and I left. We called an Uber just before midnight. We were gone before everything got really out of hand. I called my folks and said Kylie would sleep over with me, and that's what we did. We arrived home at the same time as my folks, and we all had coffee and cake together. So, as it turned out, that was a good thing. At least my parents weren't furious with me."

Maxwell let out a silent breath. Jessica wasn't the killer. She'd left, and gone home, a couple of hours before Desiree had died.

"That's lucky," he agreed. "However, we may want to question Mark to find out more about Desiree's behavior. We won't say the information came from you. We'll say we heard via the grapevine. Do you have his number and full name? Where does he live?"

"I'll message it to you. He lives in East Haven."

Jessica extricated the phone from the back pocket of her trendy ripped, rhinestone-studded jeans. Her fingers flew, and a moment later, Maxwell's phone buzzed with the incoming data.

Maxwell thought the interview had gone well, and he was pleased that he'd been able to get on Jessica's wavelength and she'd opened up to him. That was definitely thanks to him learning from Fall's intuitive questioning style. Jessica had left early and had a confirmed alibi. So she was cleared, but what she'd told him about Desiree's behavior was a game-changer.

Maxwell needed to update Stella on this, urgently. It would change the course of their investigation.

CHAPTER ELEVEN

As soon as Maxwell pulled up in the New Haven precinct parking lot, Stella jumped into the unmarked, feeling optimistic that they had a new direction that would take them further, and that they'd be investigating it together. The rain had finally stopped, and weak sunshine was doing its best to break through the clouds. The afternoon felt lighter, brighter, and more positive in every way.

"So from what Jessica said, Desiree was literally flirting, sleeping with them, and then moving on?" she confirmed.

"Yes. That seems to have been her *modus operandi*," Maxwell agreed.

"And do you think Jessica was telling the truth?" Stella glanced at Maxwell doubtfully. "She wasn't just repeating rumors?"

"The truth is a strange animal," Maxwell said as he accelerated around a corner. "Every person perceives it differently. I've learned to be suspicious of what people say and look at the motives behind their words. Given that, I do think Jessica was truthful because she admitted that Desiree had stolen her crush."

Stella nodded. "So the crush is where we're headed now?"

"Yes. Mark Halford knows we're coming. He didn't ask why we wanted to speak to him, but most probably if he did have a fling with Desiree, he might suspect it's related to that."

Stella agreed with Maxwell that Desiree had been playing a dangerous game if she'd made a habit of these brief relationships. She might have taken it lightheartedly, but what if one of the young men she'd slept with had taken it more seriously, and had felt angry and rejected when she casually moved on? What if they had found it humiliating to be 'dumped' in such a way, and had decided that they would kill in revenge?

A revenge killing wasn't something a normal person would do, Stella acknowledged. But they weren't looking for a normal person. They were looking for that one abnormal person hiding among this society, who might have been triggered by this behavior.

In fact, the killer could even have been a girlfriend whose man she had stolen, Stella thought, remembering how angry Maxwell had said

Jessica had seemed. Desiree was petite. It would not have taken a lot of strength to tighten that cable tie. It would have been more of a question of timing and nerve.

It was interesting how, as the case progressed, the layers were getting peeled back, Stella thought. The woman that had started off in their eyes as a normal parent, had then proved to be a partying divorcee, and now, was revealed as a predator who had one-night stands with men only a little older than her son.

Slowly, more and more reasons were becoming apparent for why she might have been murdered.

"Here we are. This is the road, and Mark's house is on this corner," Maxwell said, slowing the unmarked.

From Maxwell's description of Jessica, Stella had already formulated an idea of what Mark would be like. The image-conscious Jessica would most likely have been attracted by someone with looks, status, and wealth. She was pleased to see, when arriving at the lavish home, that her first suspicions were correct. Not only was Mark tall, dark, and good looking, but he was waiting for them while leaning against a silver Porsche parked in the driveway.

"Mark Halford?" Maxwell asked as they walked up to him.

With a slight smile curling his handsome mouth, he nodded.

Stella thought of asking to take this interview indoors, but then decided not to. Despite his super-confident demeanor, Mark's presence outside might mean he felt uncomfortable about being questioned within the family home. Bragging to his friends was one thing. But now, Desiree was dead, and she was sure Mark's parents didn't know what had happened between them. So, if he wanted to have this conversation while resting his elbows on the roof of his car, that was fine by her.

"We need to ask you some questions. You're not in any trouble."

Mark nodded again, as if the thought of trouble hadn't crossed his mind. His self-assurance seemed immense.

"Didn't think I was. You see, I wasn't at the party," he informed them, sounding satisfied.

He gazed at them, as if anticipating they would be stunned by this shock confession. In fact, Stella thought that Mark expected them to cut the interview short and leave.

"Why not?" Stella asked.

"I was away for the weekend. Family function. I got back Sunday evening."

"That's fortunate in light of the tragedy. But we would like to know about the background leading up to the party," she encouraged.

"There's not much to say there. I don't know anyone who could have done such a thing," he said, giving her another confident smile. "I'm not a killer and none of my friends are either, so you're not really going to be getting anything productive from us."

Stella sensed that he regarded himself as bulletproof. He'd decided that he wasn't guilty, hadn't been there, and there was no reason for him to talk. He was therefore going to stonewall them.

"Did you know the victim before her death?" she probed.

"I saw her a couple of times at parties. I mean, I knew of her. And that's really all I can say." He jingled his car keys in his hand. "Are you guys done now?"

Stella exchanged the tiniest of glances with Maxwell. They needed to drill down to the truth. It was time to start leaning on Mark and see if his enormous confidence could be dented sufficiently for him to break, and tell them the real facts.

"You about to head off somewhere?" Maxwell asked casually.

"Yeah. Soon as I'm done here, a friend and I are meeting up and going on a cross-country run," Mark said.

"You might need to postpone that run," Maxwell said conversationally.

Now Mark frowned, and his expression darkened.

"What do you mean?" he asked.

"The problem is that we need the full details of your relationship with the victim," Stella said innocently. "We're aware that there are more details and I'm hoping you can remember them. You might have left them out because you forgot about them or didn't think they were relevant."

"No, I'm not forgetting anything. Honestly," Mark protested, because now that he'd chosen his story, he had no option but to stick to it.

"It's fine. We have this happen from time to time," Stella continued calmly. "We'll simply bring you in to the interview room at the New Haven FBI headquarters for a few hours. We've found that a different environment and some alone time to think about things helps to jog the memory."

Mark was now staring at them in horror.

"Wait! You can't do that!"

Clearly, a few hours were the equivalent of life imprisonment in his mind.

"We'll tell your parents where you are, and that you're being questioned regarding your relationship with the victim," Stella said in tones that were deliberately reassuring, even though she knew that they would have exactly the opposite effect.

"No! Please! My folks – you can't tell them what goes on in my personal life!" Mark shot back.

Maxwell pounced on the words.

"That indicates there was something going on in your personal life. If you're able to recall it now, it will save us a lot of time and we won't have to make that trip," he said, with a friendly nod.

The pressure had worked. Faced with the alternative choices, Mark was more than ready to spill what he knew.

"Okay. I was – I was keeping it private out of respect to her," he explained uneasily.

"That's understandable," Stella sympathized. "However, the greatest respect we can give Desiree now is to find out who could have killed her."

"Yes. Yes. I see that. Well, I – I threw a party a couple of months ago. And she came along with a group of friends. When she found out I was the host, she flirted with me like crazy, and I flirted back. It was such a strange evening. Exciting, in a way, and – well, things reached a stage where I saw she wanted to take it further. And I was okay with that. I know she's older than me, but she was single, so I – I didn't see any harm in it."

"Absolutely," Stella encouraged.

"And, to be honest." Mark paused, shifting his feet, frowning as if grappling for the right way to voice his next words. Stella waited, giving him time.

"To be honest, I also had heard that she was – that she was a person who would do that. That she was keen. A couple of guys had talked about it in the past. They were pretty amped about it because she's hot and older; it was like a catch, they said. To have been with her."

"Was it just the once that you got together with her?" Stella asked.

"Yeah, just the once. You see, the way it was afterwards, she kind of implied that there was no need to get serious, that this was just some fun we'd had. Which was good because otherwise things might have gotten complicated," Mark explained. "This way, it was just like a really good experience."

"People are all different, though," Stella said. "You obviously understood the situation perfectly. But what if someone else hadn't?"

"As in?" Mark queried.

"As in, perhaps someone took it too seriously and fell in love or couldn't handle the rejection. Or it caused a break-up between them and their girlfriend. Something that complicated things."

Mark looked suddenly thoughtful and Stella wondered if he was thinking back to that innocent vibe he'd had with Jessica, before Desiree had burst onto the scene and derailed his attentions.

"I can't think of anyone," Mark said, but she sensed this was a reflexive response and that he had not really thought about it.

"Let's say, to finish up this interview, you have to give me three names," Stella suggested. "Three names of people who slept with her and who you think might have taken it personally or who had consequences like a break-up. Would you be able to do that?"

Mark sighed. "Look, I'm going to be in a lot of trouble if you tell people that I gave you their names."

"Have we told you who gave us your name?" Stella countered reasonably.

She watched Mark finally capitulate.

"Okay. Okay. Let me think."

He lowered his head, staring at the paving in concentration. Stella thought he was taking this seriously. He didn't want any other outcome than for them to go away and never come back. She hoped the message was clear enough that if he didn't do his part, there would be further consequences.

"I really can't give three," Mark said eventually, and his tone was now stressed. "I genuinely don't know of three. There are only four others I know she slept with. Two of them are my good friends and legit, it was just fun for them, I'd swear on it. But the other two, yes, there might have been a problem. Daniel Lomax, who lives in Guilford, can get too caught up in things. I don't know him so well, but he can be quite emotional, so just from a personality aspect, he might have had a problem with it. And I remember when we talked about it, Victor Wiseman admitted to it, but he was very quiet, and he didn't say much which is highly unusual for him. He lives two streets down from me, number twelve Maple Road."

Maxwell folded his arms.

"Thanks for those names," he said. "We're going to need your two other friends' names also. Just in case we need to rule them out at a later stage. At the moment, we need to pursue every possible lead."

"All right," Mark agreed, grimacing as if this was a betrayal of trust. "I'll message you all their contact details."

These names were a start, Stella thought. Four friends, two who had reacted in a way that could highlight a bigger problem or even a motive for murder. And since the first one lived so close by, they could drive past and see if Victor Wiseman was at home.

*

When Stella and Maxwell arrived at Victor's place, they saw he was outside, washing a car in the driveway. Stella guessed the new-looking BMW must be his personal vehicle, but even so, it surprised her how this normal activity was something that she seldom saw in this part of the world, where such things were the domain of servants and chauffeurs. It was almost dark, but in the gleam from the overhead spotlight, she could see the car looked muddy.

Victor was a stocky, cheerful-looking man with a sandy blond ponytail and tattoos on his forearms. His plaid shirtsleeves were pushed back as he soaped the red paintwork. He wore hiking boots which were also encrusted with mud.

He turned to see them, looking surprised.

"Hi, are you here for my folks? The cocktail event got moved to the Kenmuirs' place and they've already left."

He gave a second look, as if realizing that Stella and Maxwell did not, in fact, look like cocktail guests.

"We're FBI," Stella said.

Victor's eyes widened and he let go of the hose. It snaked around, sending a jet of water spraying over his jeans. Quickly he grabbed it and turned it off.

"Sorry, sorry. FBI? Seriously? Are you needing my folks?" he added, sounding worried. Then, as if recent events were catching up with him, he said, "Oh, wait. This must be in connection with the murder?"

Victor then, very helpfully, blushed crimson, physically confirming that there was a link between him and the deceased woman.

Stella could see that this guy had a mouth that ran a little way ahead of his brain. That was a useful trait, and it meant there was no need for a soft approach.

"We're seeking background," she said. "Were you at the party where it happened?"

Victor nodded. "Yes, but only for a couple of hours. I went early and left at eleven."

"Why?" Maxwell asked.

"Because my folks were at a wedding. They said they would be back sometime after midnight, and I was kind of supposed to be looking after my younger sister, but she's sixteen and pretty good at looking after herself, so I snuck out and then I snuck back and nobody ever knew. Thank goodness I was gone before things got – got complicated. Or I'd have been grounded for a year," he said, making a rueful face. "I guess I shouldn't be telling you this. Too much info, right?"

"Can you prove you left at that time?" Stella asked.

"Yeah. My folks got home at one and can confirm I was in the games room. They looked in on me to say hi."

"We're here for some other information also," Stella said.

Victor's face fell. "You heard I had a fling with her? That was months ago. At least two months. It was only the once. There's no way I killed her! You can't suspect me because that happened, or else you'll have to suspect half of Connecticut. Sorry. That was disrespectful," he concluded, sounding abashed.

"We've heard that you didn't talk much about it and that you were very quiet when the matter was discussed between groups of friends. What did this affair mean to you?"

It was all the more suspicious since Victor was clearly a motor mouth.

"Oh, yeah. Yeah. I learned my lesson on that a while ago," he said.

"How do you mean?" Maxwell challenged him.

"Well, I found out that some people – one person, to be exact, got very upset when it was mentioned."

"Explain, please?" Stella said.

"The subject came up when I and a group of friends were out having drinks. And I did shoot my mouth off, and everyone seemed fascinated by my story, but boy I got into trouble from Daniel Lomax. He was furious. I mean, so furious he tried to hit me. He told me to shut up and be respectful, and that my behavior was disgusting, and then he stormed out."

"Is that so?" Stella asked. Now Daniel had been mentioned twice. Both Victor and Mark had confirmed him to be emotionally invested in the relationship with Desiree, and a person who overreacted.

"Yeah. That's what happened. So after that, I made sure not to talk about it, because I realized that some people, like Daniel, might have gotten too involved during the fling. Which I don't understand because really, it was all just good fun with no strings. She was honest about it."

"Was Daniel at the party?"

Victor thought, frowning.

"Yes. I saw him there, but I didn't speak to him. Especially with her there, after what happened, I thought it was best to keep out of his way."

"Do you know where Daniel lives?" Stella asked, hoping that it was close by if he was in their circle of friends.

"He's with his mother in the week. She lives in Stratford. She's Dr. Lomax, actually," Victor elaborated. "Some kind of surgeon."

"Thanks for your help," Stella said. "I'd appreciate if you didn't call anyone to tell them about this. It will be better for the investigation if we can go ahead without anyone knowing who we plan to speak to."

"No, no. I wouldn't do that anyway. And please don't tell anyone I told you the name," Victor appealed.

With confidentiality on both sides ensured, they left.

Stella hoped that the threads of this investigation would start to twist together now, and that the scanty information would start forming a pattern. Daniel could be an important part of the pattern. In fact, his extreme reaction could provide the only clue they still needed.

CHAPTER TWELVE

It was fully dark by the time Stella and Maxwell pulled up outside the timber-fronted house in a quiet area of Stratford, with a neat front yard and immaculate board fencing separating its sizeable grounds from the neighbors.

Stella hoped that Daniel would be inside, watching television or playing online games, and blissfully unaware of their arrival until it was too late. They needed the element of surprise, and for him to be unprepared.

She hoped this lead would finally mean progress. It felt like they were casting around, but coming up against weak suspects, or alibis, every time. She remembered Detective Grover's warning words and feared they would prove prophetic.

This case couldn't go cold! Surely it couldn't? Surely Desiree's reckless behavior would eventually lead the way to her killer's identity, if they were able to follow the trail?

She knocked on the door and waited. In a few moments, footsteps approached. A young man dressed in sweats and sneakers opened the door with an expectant look on his face.

"Hey," he began, and then stopped.

The expression on his face – which was lean, with a hint of dark stubble – turned to confusion, and then to horror, as he saw them.

Stella wondered who he'd been about to greet. He'd clearly been expecting someone.

"We're from the FBI. Are you Daniel Lomax?"

Stella assumed from the widening of his eyes that this was, in fact, his name. He stared at them for a long, silent moment. He looked terrified. Then, abruptly, he slammed the door in their faces. The panicked slap of his shoes on the tiled corridor faded into the distance.

"Open up!" Maxwell yelled, ramming his shoulder against the door.

There were only two possibilities, Stella thought. Either Daniel was going to hide in the house, or else he was making a run for it, and hoping to get a head start.

Stella's money was on running. His panicked demeanor and the haste of his footsteps told her this was the decision he'd choose. And in that case, she needed to cut off his escape routes.

"I'll go around," Stella shouted.

Turning away from the door, she raced across the front yard, heading around the house.

She pounded over the lawn, her shoes digging into the soft, wet grass as she dodged between flower beds and under an archway draped with climbing roses. This time of year, there were no blooms visible. The dull green leaves brushed wetly against her hair.

A chest-high steel-barred fence separated the front of the house from the back. The padlock on the gate gleamed in the sudden glow of a security light that must have been activated by her movement.

Without breaking stride, Stella rested her palms on top of the curved steel bars and used her speed to propel herself into a high, desperate vault. The narrow rails bit into her palms. Bruising pain lanced into her hands as she shoved herself up and over. She thumped down onto her feet, staggered, rebalanced, and then continued.

The back of the house contained a large swimming pool, as well as a covered patio with tables and chairs set out. Muted spotlights glowed from the roof and walls, making the pristine setup look like a show house waiting to be photographed.

The sliding door leading onto the patio was partway open. Did that mean Daniel was already out? Breathing hard, she looked around the large backyard. The split-pole fence separating this property from the one behind was climbable, but the yard was large. Could he have gotten all the way across the grass, and over it, so quickly?

Or was he hiding somewhere, waiting for her to go looking inside, so he could make a sprint for the back fence, and be over and away?

Stella guessed he was hiding. She didn't think he would have had time to run the whole way across the lawn and scale the fence, and she could see no footprints on the wet grass. She tiptoed toward the patio. Where could he be?

There was a tree ahead, and a well-trimmed topiary hedge beyond. To her right was a wooden shed, where she guessed some of the pool equipment and accessories might be kept.

Her breath sounded loud in her own ears. She could feel her heart thumping. Her ears strained for any sound, but only picked up the rustle of leaves in the chilly wind. In the glow of the spotlights, the leaves were casting moving shadows that distracted her. Would she pick up in time if he made a run for it, in this semi-darkness?

"Mr. Lomax, this is only getting you into worse trouble. We need to speak to you," Stella called, her voice firm.

She listened for any response or reaction to her words but couldn't pick up any sound. She paused, waiting, doing her best to connect herself with her surroundings and tune out the gusting, rustling background.

Then she moved on, glancing again at the sliding door. He could have doubled back inside. He could be waiting anywhere.

Stella tensed as she heard a crash from the far side of the house. That meant Maxwell had gotten in the front door. He would immediately begin searching the house. If Daniel was hiding inside, Maxwell would flush him out.

His options were narrowing. He would act in panic, soon. He would have to, and she needed to be ready.

She jumped as she saw a shadowy form to her right, beyond the hedge, but it was only a shrub that had been pruned down for winter, its twisted branches resembling limbs.

He must be in the shed. It was the only place.

Stella wished the wind would die down so she could pick up small noises. Like Daniel breathing. That would be a useful sound. The weather was helping him, not her.

She grabbed the shed door. She was going to have to act like Maxwell. Fast, aggressive, and ready for anything.

As Stella braced herself, ready to pull it open, the gangly man exploded out from behind the shed.

In a rush, he burst past her. His flailing arm struck her painfully in her midriff, knocking the breath out of her. The blow was unintentional, but it slowed her down.

He was going to get away. Gasping for air, Stella launched herself in pursuit. He could not get away. He could not!

He made for the back fence, and she followed him, yelling, "Stop! FBI!"

As they raced across the lawn, Stella realized in utter frustration that she was not close enough to catch him. The tall, long-legged man would be able to grab the fence and vault over before she reached it. And she would be slower, scrambling over those high, sheer boards.

She couldn't stop him. But she might be able to make him think she could. Mind games could be a powerful weapon and right now, they were the only one she had.

"You're not going to make it over that fence," she yelled as loud as she could. "I'm right behind you. I'm going to catch you. I have a gun!"

The mention of the gun caused Daniel to break stride. He glanced around at her.

That hesitation had given her enough time, and she would be able to grab him as he climbed. Stella saw him realize it. Lightning-quick, he changed his plan. He veered away from the fence and raced in the other direction. Swerving left, she chased him as fast as she could.

He looked to be taking the same route she had done, going the other way. His plan must be to vault right over that steel fence, charge out of the front yard, and lose them in the darkness of the quiet street.

At that moment, Maxwell ran out of the house through the sliding door. She saw him, a dark, wiry shape silhouetted against the muted light.

"FBI! Stop running!" he yelled.

Hearing the sound of his voice, Daniel froze again and then found his stride once more, racing past the pool.

That momentary pause brought Stella within fingertip-reach of him. Suddenly, with focused clarity, she knew what she needed to do.

She dove forward, and her fingers closed on the back of Daniel's flapping sweatshirt. Grabbing the fold of fabric as firmly as she could, Stella tugged it sideways with all her strength.

Her efforts succeeded beyond her wildest expectations. She'd hoped to make him stumble so she could tackle him from behind. But Daniel slipped on the smooth, wet tiles and cartwheeled to the left. With an almighty splash, he somersaulted into the pool.

Stella sprawled down as water cascaded out, splattering coldly over her face and splashing over the smooth granite tiles. Maxwell ran to the opposite side of the pool, effectively bracketing their now drenched and spluttering target.

Stella clambered to her feet. Her pants were soaked and she was going to have bruises on both knees, but it was worth it. They'd stopped Daniel from escaping. Now, trapped in the pool, he had nowhere to go but out, and straight into their custody.

Daniel climbed slowly out on Maxwell's side. Cold water streamed from his clothes, and he was shivering. His face looked pinched and remorseful. He was clearly regretting his actions, but even so, Maxwell wasn't taking any chances. Immediately, Maxwell grasped his arm firmly.

"I – I'm sorry. I – I thought – I thought, er –," Daniel's voice tailed off. Clearly, he could not, in fact, come up with any plausible reason why he might have decided to run.

Glancing at the waters of the pool, Stella noticed something floating there. It was a twisted plastic bag with a sleeve of tablets inside, and she guessed it must have fallen out of Daniel's pockets during his impromptu swim.

"What's that?" she asked, pointing to it.

Daniel spun around. His gaze locked onto the floating bag, and then veered toward Stella, and she saw he was now looking even more disturbed.

"I – I don't know," he muttered, and Stella guessed the shake in his voice wasn't only due to his cold dunking.

Crouching down on the wet tiles, she leaned out, and was able to grab the plastic between her index and middle fingers. Carefully, she lifted it out of the water and stood.

Maxwell looked at the bag and then, more sternly, at the white-faced Daniel.

"Come with us," he said. "You're in big trouble. And you have a lot of answers to give us now."

CHAPTER THIRTEEN

Half an hour later, Stella and Maxwell were sitting opposite Daniel, in one of the New Haven interview rooms. They had allowed Daniel to change into dry clothes, but he was still shivering. Stella guessed it was more from fear than cold, but all the same, Maxwell had fetched him a blanket. He clutched it around him as he regarded them apprehensively.

Maxwell had placed the plastic bag on the table next to Daniel's phone. The plastic gleamed in the harsh overhead lights.

"Where is your mother tonight?" was Stella's first question.

Daniel flinched at the word.

"She's at work. She's operating on a patient. She said she'll be back around midnight."

"You were expecting somebody else to arrive when we got there. Who?"

"A – a friend."

"For that?" Stella pointed to the plastic bag.

The fact that the friend hadn't knocked on the door, after seeing a typical police unmarked parked in the driveway, told her a lot about this person. Most likely, he'd abandoned the deal and made a run for it.

Daniel stared at the floor, looking as if his world had ended.

Stella picked up the bag.

"It's not what you think," Daniel squeaked, his voice panicked.

"It looks to me like uppers. Party drugs. So you can dance all night. How did you get hold of these for your 'friend?'" Stella asked. When Daniel didn't answer, she added, "Would having a mother with a prescription notepad have made this easier?"

"Please don't put me in jail," Daniel muttered.

Stella exchanged a glance with Maxwell.

Daniel was clearly guilty. The question was now: to what extent?

Maxwell spoke, in a harsh voice.

"Tell me about your relationship with Desiree Jardine," he said.

Daniel looked at him, an appalled expression spreading across his face.

"Now is not the moment to lie," Maxwell warned. "You've wasted enough of our time already."

"Okay, okay, I had – I had a – a short relationship with her," Daniel said.

"When was that?"

"In September. We met up on a weekend in September."

"Who ended it?"

"She did. I – okay, I got more involved than I should have. I hoped it would last. But she said that it had just been a fun weekend. Nothing more."

"Were you angry?"

"I was upset. I guess I thought it was more serious, and that we'd be together for longer. I mean, I know the age difference is a thing, but I didn't think it mattered. So yes, I was upset for a while. Not angry."

"Really?" Disbelief dripped from Maxwell's words. It was clear he was far from convinced, and Daniel fumbled to present his side more coherently.

"I respected Desiree. I mean, I was gutted when it ended, but I wouldn't speak badly of her. Or allow anyone else to. People called her some horrible names. I didn't think that was fair. Why should other guys be allowed to call – to call a woman easy, or a slut? Why her and not you? If you slept with her, what does that make you? That's what my feeling is."

Daniel's voice was jittery, his words fragmented, but Stella couldn't help agreeing with his sentiment. What he said was very true.

In fact, Daniel's words were resonating with her, and Stella had a fleeting, but definite thought there might be a bigger picture to be seen if she followed this line of logic.

Filing that idea away for now, she continued with the questioning.

"Were you at the party on Saturday?" she asked.

"Yes. I saw Desiree there but I – I got upset all over again when I saw her flirting with other guys. It made me feel very angry and kind of unwanted. Like I didn't belong there. It was a horrible feeling. So I left. I think it was about eleven p.m. by then. I didn't want to go home. I messaged another friend instead."

"Really?" Stella asked. Daniel could have lost his temper and acted in a moment of rage. Or, more coldly, have devised a plan to help that horrible feeling go away. He was dealing in prescription drugs. He'd run when they arrived, he'd lied, and she didn't believe him.

"Prove it," she insisted.

"Okay, I will. I will. We went clubbing in New Haven and got back at about five in the morning. We Ubered there and back because we were already both drunk. I can show you the record on my phone if you like. The messages I sent to my friend, before I arrived there. I can show you those. And I ordered the Uber coming back."

He stared at them anxiously, as if hoping that the responsible decision not to drive drunk might outweigh the fact that he'd been forging prescriptions to supply his friends with party drugs.

"Show us," Stella said.

Daniel reached for his phone and scrolled anxiously through.

"Here. It's here. You see?"

Leaning over his shoulder, Stella looked at the messages, which were sent at eleven-fifteen p.m. on Saturday night.

"Hey, you want to go to New Haven? This party is boring."

"Serious? I have to study this weekend."

"Study next weekend. I'll pay 4 us to get into Legends."

"Okay, deal!"

"CU in 20!"

Then, Daniel swiped through his phone to display the return trip. It proved that on the night of Desiree's murder, Daniel had Ubered from a club in downtown New Haven, to his friend's residential address, at four-fifteen a.m.

"I've got some photos I uploaded on social media, that I took while we were there. I'll show you those, too."

He scrolled again, his hands shaking.

So, despite having been hurt and angry after Desiree had broken off their fleeting relationship, he was cleared as the killer because her death had occurred between two and four a.m.

But there was still the issue that he'd been providing, or selling, prescription drugs.

"Your mother's only back after midnight?" Stella asked.

"That's correct," Daniel said apprehensively.

Stella glanced at Maxwell. She wasn't sure what to do in this situation. Daniel had been an honest witness. But he'd also been a drugs supplier.

Maxwell took his phone and scrolled through.

"Dad," he said, sounding satisfied. "This is your father, right?"

"It is. But please, don't –"

Maxwell was already dialing.

"Hello. Mr. Lomax?" he asked. "Yes. This is Agent Maxwell, from the FBI. I'm calling because we arrived to question your son for a case we're handling. He cooperated with us in the questioning. However, we found prescription drugs on his person. He's currently in the New Haven FBI office."

Maxwell paused, listening to the outpouring of words from the other side of the line. Catching some of the shouted conversation, Stella picked up that Mr. Lomax was absolutely furious with his son.

"Lock him up!" she heard him shout. "That'll teach him!"

"No, sir. We won't arrest him, as we're investigating a murder and this was an incidental issue," Maxwell said. "However, if he continues this way, he'll be in big trouble. We'll take him back to his mother's house now, and you can meet him there."

He waited, listened.

"Great. Half an hour? We'll be waiting. Oh, and you might want to call a locksmith out. The front door needs some repairs."

He turned to Daniel, looking satisfied as he gave him back his phone. Stella was filled with admiration at the fair and effective way he'd handled the situation. Daniel, on the other hand, looked appalled at the disastrous turn his evening had taken.

Stella hoped that this experience would put him off doing any further dealings. It was a step along the road to crime. It didn't take many steps to start becoming one of the bad guys. And there were more than enough of them, without a reckless, opportunistic twenty-one-year-old adding to their numbers.

What he'd said in Desiree's defense had stuck in Stella's mind. His words had felt significant, and Stella knew she'd briefly leaped along a chain of logic that was relevant to the case. Unfortunately, the thought had been so fleeting, and the link so tenuous, she couldn't work out exactly where it led.

If they didn't get results on this case soon, Roth was going to start doubting their capabilities. If she and Maxwell were to be entrusted with another solo case any time soon, Stella knew that by tomorrow, they would have to find answers.

She tried to reassure herself by remembering that tomorrow morning, Desiree's call records would be available, as well as the toxicology report, and they could read through the case file. Hopefully, some clues to her killer might be hidden there.

CHAPTER FOURTEEN

At nine-thirty p.m., just as they were leaving Daniel's house, Stella heard Maxwell's phone start ringing.

He glanced down at the car's display and made a frustrated face.

"It's Roth," he said. He glanced at Stella, and she knew he shared all the worries she'd been internalizing. "Better get this over with," he decided, punching the answer button. A moment later, Roth's voice filled the car.

"Haven't had an update from you or Fall today. What's been happening?"

"Groundwork today," Maxwell said shortly. "We're driving back to New Haven now."

"Groundwork?" Roth asked, sounding less than pleased.

"Getting foundations in place. Fact finding. No real progress," Maxwell admitted, and Stella knew as he spoke them how those words burned. She felt incredibly inadequate that there was nothing to report.

"No firm suspects as yet, from a simple house party?" Roth sounded surprised. Hearing that in his voice made it even worse.

"It wasn't simple," Stella tried to explain.

"What do you mean by that, Fall?" Roth asked.

"The party was totally out of control. Hordes of uninvited guests showed up, and because there was so much underage drinking, a lot of people fled in the morning as soon as they realized there was trouble. We've managed to get a list of about twenty people confirmed as being there. We're working our way through the list. We've ruled out the ex-husband that Desiree divorced a few months ago. We've ruled out a few of her young lovers."

"Young lovers?" Roth asked.

Maxwell answered. "Desiree had a habit of seducing the younger guys. She was known for it. Had earned herself quite a reputation. That's how she must have ended up at the party."

Roth was quiet for a few minutes.

"That is more complex than I expected," he admitted.

"We've got more information coming in tomorrow. We should have the toxicology report by then, and have viewed the case file," Stella said.

"I also asked the police to pull her recent calls," Maxwell said.

"Why haven't you viewed the case file already?" Roth asked, sounding surprised.

Stella exchanged another glance with Maxwell.

"Detective Grover is being obstructive," she said.

There was a pause.

"Why's he being obstructive?" Now Roth sounded impatient, as if he'd expected Stella and Maxwell to have the necessary people skills to get past this problem.

"He told us upfront that the case is likely to go cold, because there's such a small chance of figuring out who was at the party and could have done it. He says similar cases in the past have done the same. I don't know why he's being so difficult," Stella said, hearing the frustration loud in her own voice. "Perhaps he has a preconceived idea that none of the local boys could have done such a thing, and he's not keen to make trouble for them. Perhaps he's worried the FBI will solve the case, which will make him look bad with two similar cold cases on his books."

"It's annoying when that happens. But you need to work around it, work with his team, and build a partnership. Don't be shy to ask for help from them."

"We're trying to do exactly that," Stella reassured Roth. "Tomorrow morning we'll be at the Putnam precinct. The case file will be ready, and we'll also have some help with interviewing witnesses and following up on Desiree's calls."

"Okay. I can see you have had a few bumps to smooth out," Roth said dubiously.

"There'll be more to report by end of day tomorrow," Maxwell said in firm tones.

"All right," Roth agreed, but he still sounded far from happy. "By then, I need to see some results. Or else I'll have to leave Agent Billings and work with you on this."

That was more of a threat than a promise, Stella knew. They couldn't afford another day of no progress. It wouldn't reflect well on them, and Roth would rightly start questioning their capabilities.

Maxwell disconnected.

"Well, that was fun," he said cynically.

"I feel so ashamed," Stella said. "How can we have done so badly, Maxwell? Have we been unlucky, or genuinely missing something? Every lead we've had so far has fizzled out."

Maxwell sighed. "Welcome to 'A Normal Day in the Life of an Investigator.'"

Stella gave a reluctant smile, feeling the misery inside her untwist just a little.

"This is par for the course," Maxwell reassured her. "So is being hassled by superiors who aren't working on the case. Roth's just on our backs because he's not here. If he was here, he'd understand the situation better."

"We need to make an early start tomorrow," Stella said, feeling the pressure weighing heavy on her.

"Yeah, we do. I'll tell you what. Let me drop you home now. Your place is closer than the New Haven office. Then I can pick you up in the morning and we head straight out again. That'll save some time. How does that sound?"

"That sounds good," Stella said. "Thanks."

With the late flight back from Colorado yesterday, and the long drive from JFK Airport to her home, she was short on sleep, and only now realizing how tiredness weighed her down.

"We need to eat. Can I buy you some food as a thank-you?" Stella asked.

"Food? Now that's a great idea," Maxwell said.

The day had been so busy, neither of them had had a moment to eat. At least Roth couldn't accuse them of wasting any time on a lunch break, Stella thought.

"There's an Italian place across the road from me," she suggested. "They do fantastic pasta. We could stop there quickly."

"I'll take you up on that for sure," Maxwell said enthusiastically.

As he navigated the streets into downtown New Haven, Stella found herself looking forward to dinner with Maxwell. Of course, now that they were in the middle of a pressurized case, it would be strictly a working dinner, and not a date. The last dinner they'd been on had definitely been a date. But apart from wanting to take it slow, she needed to separate her work life from any budding romance.

Late-evening traffic was light as Maxwell sped through the streets and parked outside the Italian place. It was just a block from Stella's house. Live opera music resonated from inside as they headed to the door. Stella loved the music. It lifted her heart. She wasn't sure if Maxwell liked opera and glanced at him anxiously.

He was looking amped.

"This is so cool," he said as they headed in.

The tables were all full, but as they arrived, a couple was vacating one of the couches in the bar area.

"You want to sit there?" the waitress asked.

"Sure," Maxwell said."

She led them across the crowded restaurant, and they sat down side by side on the comfortable couch, which had a low table in front of it.

"Perfect for a quick meal," Maxwell said.

Stella scanned the menu hungrily. They placed their orders for food, and a glass of red wine each.

"Roth said you were out of town yesterday," Maxwell said. "Did you go anywhere interesting?"

Stella hesitated before replying.

There wasn't any way to get around this innocent question. Maxwell was her partner, and there was a romantic spark between them. He deserved to know where she'd been. He didn't deserve anything less than the truth.

Maxwell knew there were issues with her family and that she'd grown up with only her mother, but she hadn't told him more than that. Was she going to be able to talk about it? So few people knew. It was easier not to tell, and to protect herself by keeping the painful story a secret. What if people didn't believe her? What if they criticized and insulted her father for his actions, the same way her mother had done again and again over those lonely years that followed? What if they said Stella was in denial, and he must be dead?

Her best friend Rebecca, who'd known her since they were in junior high school, knew everything Stella had been through. Clem, her mentor, knew most of her back story. Those two people were the only two she had trusted enough to tell.

Now, she was surprised that she felt ready to unburden to a third. She sensed that Maxwell would believe her and that he would understand. More than that, she felt she owed it to him. After all, they were getting closer, and to hold such an important part of her life back from him would be wrong.

Squashed against him on the cozy couch, Stella found herself feeling more confident than she'd expected. For some reason, being side by side made it less daunting to speak.

"I got a lead on my dad," she said.

"How do you mean?" Maxwell turned to her. His face was a picture as he struggled to understand exactly what Stella meant by that strange statement.

"He disappeared when I was ten. He went missing. One day, he never came home."

"From work? Or what happened?" Maxwell asked, sounding concerned.

"From work," Stella confirmed.

Maxwell blinked as he took in this curveball.

"What did he do?" he asked after a pause.

"He was a detective in a Kansas precinct."

"And nobody knew where he'd gone?" Maxwell said incredulously.

"Nobody knew anything. He left work and vanished, they said."

Now Maxwell's face was taut with concern.

"That must have been hell for you."

"It was. I cried every night, thinking about what might have happened to him. I couldn't understand why my mother didn't do more to find him. Why she didn't move heaven and earth to discover where he'd gone. I thought – did she really hate him so much that she doesn't care? And deep down, I felt sure that he couldn't be dead. That he must still be alive, somehow, somewhere."

She felt a catharsis as she spilled the story out, sharing some of the pain she kept hidden deep inside.

"That's hectic, Stella."

Maxwell was using her first name. At work, they addressed each other by last names. But now, things felt more personal.

"Eventually, my mother sent me this address in Colorado. So I went there on Sunday morning, to see if he still lived there. He didn't. He'd moved on. The neighbors sent me his last known phone number, but it's out of service now. So I'm still looking."

Maxwell was looking at her with a strange expression, half curiosity, half sympathy.

"Do you know why he disappeared? That's such a weird thing to do. I guess that must have defined your life, in a way."

"Yes. I think it did shape me as a person. I would have preferred to be shaped by more positive things, but I couldn't choose, and I don't know why he vanished. My mother said he abandoned us. Things were not great between them."

"But to up and leave is radically extreme," Maxwell said. Stella could see he was feeling his way through the conversation and that he didn't want to speak badly of her father.

"I wondered if he had a mental breakdown," Stella confessed. "He didn't seem that way. He always impressed me as a stable person, but I was just a kid. What did I know?"

"Did you ever think it might be related to a case he was working on?" Maxwell suggested.

Stella stared at him in surprise.

She had never considered that with any seriousness – until now.

Perhaps it was only now, faced with the weight and implications of what every case meant for her own career, that she could see it might be a possibility. As a child she hadn't understood the seriousness of what a criminal investigation could mean. Even though that scenario had briefly crossed her mind, she'd discounted it immediately and hadn't revisited the idea since.

But still – a detective in a small, suburban police station in Kansas? What could he have come across that would have prompted a need for such a drastic, irreversible step?

"I never really did until now; I didn't understand how complex cases could be," she admitted.

At that moment, their food and wine arrived. They'd both ordered the Bolognese – filling comfort food. The steaming pasta and rich, meaty sauce smelled beyond delicious. Stella's stomach was growling so loudly that she felt glad the opera music was playing, to drown it out.

"Maybe you could find out somehow," Maxwell encouraged, once the plates had been set out in front of them. "If nothing else, doing some research would give you a picture of what he did, and what he had dealt with every working day. I think that would be good."

Something about the wistful way he spoke made Stella decide to ask him a similar question.

"Your father? Did you have a good relationship with him?" she asked.

Maxwell shrugged. "I never knew him. He died when I was young. No mystery there. He was killed in a car wreck on the way to work. He worked as a builder on construction sites, and the guys used to travel in the back of the truck, all crammed together, and the truck overturned and rolled. He was killed instantly. Three of the men were. The others weren't as lucky and survived for a while with horrific injuries."

"Rick, that's awful. How old were you? Were you old enough to know?"

"I was four. Yeah, old enough to remember the devastation. For all of us. I missed him terribly. I don't have many memories of him, but I remember him being very tall, and very caring. That's not a lot to go on, but it's all I had," he said sadly.

"How did your mother cope without him?" Stella asked, remembering her own tough, joyless childhood after her dad's disappearance.

"My mother was destroyed. They really loved each other. The light of her life had gone. And obviously, it was a disaster financially as well. He didn't earn much, but he was the major breadwinner. I'm the middle child of three. My mother had to provide for us on her own."

"What did she do?" Stella asked.

"She worked as a cleaner. She took on additional weekend shifts. And then she got a night job, as a receptionist in a hospital four nights a week. She worked herself to the bone, but she never, ever complained. She was a happy, positive role model. I don't know how she managed it. All three of us grew up with a blazing determination to make a success of our lives and to repay her for what she did. Today, she doesn't work anymore. We all banded together and bought her a little place in Scottsville, Arizona, close to where her mother lives. It's a real friendly community. She has a dog and a cat. I think she's even dating again. We look after her."

"That's amazing," Stella said. She'd been caught up in Maxwell's story, fascinated by the glimpse into his own past that he was finally giving her.

She scraped up the final, tasty mouthful of her food. This didn't feel like a date, she decided, not while they were battling with such a serious investigation. But in a way, it felt better than a date. It felt like finally she'd gotten to know more about the person that Maxwell really was.

She hadn't told him everything and she felt sure that he was also holding things back. But at least they knew more about each other's formative experiences.

Stella felt a weird mix of happiness and terror as she thought about being able to have an actual relationship with somebody again one day. Could she trust enough? If she did, Maxwell seemed like a person she could trust, and having that thought felt as if a painful barrier in her mind was starting to release.

"I've been wanting to do this for a while with you, Stella," he said.

Stella nodded. "Music?" she asked.

"No," Maxwell sounded slightly amused. "Not music. Getting to know you better. And this has been a good chance. I know you don't like talking about yourself."

"Nor do you," Stella pointed out. They were alike in that way.

"True," Maxwell agreed. She saw his expression harden for a moment and guessed there was more she'd have to find out that he hadn't yet told her.

"I guess we should get some rest now," Stella said.

"I guess so," Maxwell said, but he didn't move and nor did she. She felt warm, squashed against Maxwell's jacket in this calm, opera-infused place. Everyone around them was enjoying themselves, carefree. For a moment, Stella felt just like one of them. Maxwell reached out and slid his arm around her. Stella rested her head on his shoulder.

It was the closest they'd been. It felt right. Stella's mind was whirling. She still felt afraid, and there was good reason for that after her disastrous engagement. But she also felt hopeful. There was no abyss between her and Maxwell's circumstances. She could understand the way Maxwell thought, and how he'd fought to overcome adversity. She admired his kindness to his mother, and she had huge respect for the integrity and sharp professionalism that shone from him at work.

And yet, she couldn't suppress the terror that the man she was starting to get so emotionally involved with might still turn out to be someone other than she thought.

You can't keep having your life ruled by fear, Stella told herself firmly. This is the moment. Seize it. Show your feelings. Stop being so afraid of letting yourself be known and be loved.

As she reached out to clasp his hand, feeling his fingers link warmly into hers, Stella felt, with a sense of breathless happiness, that at least one thing had finally gone right on this discouraging day.

By tomorrow evening, she hoped they would have more answers. Solving this case, and proving Grover wrong, would be crucial – for Roth, for herself, and for Maxwell.

CHAPTER FIFTEEN

Stella was woken early the next morning by the shrill ringing of her phone. It tore her from her fragmented dreams. Even though she'd been exhausted, she'd had difficulty getting to sleep. Surprisingly, after the dinner with Maxwell, she had struggled with nightmares. She'd dreamed of falling asleep nestled against him, only to wake, screaming, as she turned to face the staring, empty eyes of her ex-fiancé, the blood spatters dark on his greenish-pale skin.

Stella grabbed her phone, glad that its sound had ripped her out of this emotionally shredding cycle.

It was Spencer Glenn, the pathologist, on the line.

"Agent Fall? Sorry to call you so early. I just got the toxicology results from Mrs. Jardine's tests."

The tox results? Stella sat up, excitement sharpening her focus. If Glenn was calling so early, it meant there was something significant to be found in them.

"Her alcohol level was 0.14 percent. So she'd had a few drinks, but not a life-threatening amount of alcohol. But we also found traces of cocaine in her blood," he said.

Cocaine?

Stella scrambled to her feet. This was unexpected. None of the other students at the party had mentioned cocaine. Stella didn't think they'd been lying or omitting the information. They had drunk themselves into a stupor and had admitted to that freely.

But cocaine? Where had Desiree obtained it from, Stella wondered.

It was another layer of darkness revealed. Involvement in hard drugs could have provided a motive for the murder.

"Thanks, Glenn," she said. "We'll follow up on that straight away, and hopefully it will progress this case."

"I hope so," he said somberly.

Immediately when she'd said goodbye, Stella called Maxwell.

"Morning, Maxwell," she said.

"Morning, Fall," he replied. At the start of a pressured working day, they were back on a last-name basis. Stella didn't want it different. The formality reassured her, and she sensed that he felt the same.

"Desiree Jardine had cocaine in her bloodstream," she said quickly.

"Interesting," Maxwell said, his voice sharp. "Now where would she have obtained that from? A friend? Direct from a dealer, perhaps?"

"We need to find out."

"We can start by going through her calls and messages. I asked Jansen to pull her call records yesterday and those should have come through by now. We can print them out there, take a look, and view the file at Putnam. Then we'll have some help with the case as well. I'll pick you up in twenty minutes?"

"I'll be waiting," Stella said. She cut the call and sprinted for the shower.

*

They arrived at the Putman precinct at nine.

Stella's first impression was that this was a typical suburban precinct. It looked somewhat shabby, as if it was due for a refurbishment. There were planters on either side of the main door, but they had nothing growing in them. The paving on the left of the parking lot was uneven, as if it had been damaged by frost or water and not yet repaired.

Inside, the young sergeant glanced curiously at them.

"Morning," Maxwell said. "FBI agents Maxwell and Fall, working on the Jardine case. Can we go through and meet with Detective Grover?"

"Is he expecting you?" the sergeant asked dubiously.

"He should be," Maxwell said.

The sergeant picked up the phone and dialed. He spoke briefly and then nodded.

"Okay. You can go through."

He got up from his desk and unlocked the interleading door.

Stella walked behind the sergeant into the back office. It was a hive of activity. She saw Jansen first. He was speaking urgently into the phone, looking stressed.

"I will await your urgent response. You'll get back to me as soon as you can? Yes, this is a priority. I need answers on it as soon as possible. No, this afternoon won't be ideal. Can you get it for me this morning?"

At least they were taking the case seriously, and moving on it, Stella thought in relief. She'd been worried yesterday but had clearly misjudged Grover. Now she felt bad about her own negative thoughts and comments. It was reassuring to see that the investigation department was now so involved. She remembered Roth's advice about cooperating and working together. With luck, their combined resources could help to solve this case as fast as possible.

As she thought about Grover, she saw him, in a glassed-off cubicle beyond the main office. He, too, was speaking rapidly on the phone while a cigarette smoldered in an ashtray next to him.

Jansen put the phone down and turned to Stella and Maxwell, but before he could speak a word or even greet them, the phone started ringing again and he grabbed it.

"Detective Jansen," he said hurriedly. He listened, and then picked up a pen.

"Yes, absolutely. Yes, it's a priority case. That information will be essential to us. You'll send it through now? Thank you."

Finally, he replaced the phone once more, and was able to speak to Stella and Maxwell.

"Good morning," he said.

"Morning. It sounds like you're making progress on the case? What information is arriving?" Stella said.

Jansen looked embarrassed.

"Actually, I – er –" he began, but was interrupted by a loud throat clearing as Grover emerged from his smoking cubicle.

"Morning, agents," he said, in rapid tones. "We've got an emergency situation here. A local resident was carjacked early this morning and left by the side of the road in critical condition. We've got information that the fugitives robbed a local convenience store an hour ago and held the proprietor at gunpoint. My entire team is urgently following up on all available leads."

Stella stared at him in utter shock.

It wasn't as if a carjacking and robbery were not serious crimes. Of course they were. But so serious that every resource had to be pulled away from other crimes, and reallocated to it? Including from a murder investigation?

"What about the Jardine case?" she asked. She had to stop her voice from shaking. She didn't know if it was more from anger, or from shock.

"It's not the same level of priority. We have armed fugitives at large, at this moment, endangering the lives of our community. Once this situation is contained, we can, of course, look at reallocating our resources," Grover said. He was bristling with self-importance. His air of authority was tangible.

Stella exchanged a disbelieving glance with Maxwell.

"You have a whole unit here. Is there nobody who can work with us?" Maxwell asked incredulously.

"Are you telling me how to run my precinct?" Grover shot back, all his bullying qualities now clearly visible. "We have local lives at risk. My priority is to manage this threat. If you interfere, I'm reporting you to your superior," he sneered.

Maxwell turned away, shaking his head, and Stella saw it was taking every inch of his self-control to defuse the situation and be the more mature person. Grover was clearly spoiling for a fight, hoping they would lose control and that he would then have real ammunition to use against them. Maxwell wasn't going to give him any leverage and nor was she.

It was abundantly clear that Grover was pulling resources off their case because the FBI had become involved without his say-so. Also, Stella was increasingly suspicious that he must have personal reasons for not wanting to prioritize it.

Never mind working with the local police department. They weren't going to be able to do that at all. They were on their own on this case, and it couldn't be more of a catastrophe.

Support from the local detectives, with their knowledge of the area, was always a given. It could go far in speeding things up, especially with the long list of partygoers they still had to question, in addition to the new drugs angle.

Grover was abandoning them, and Desiree Jardine.

Radiating officiousness, Grover hurried back into his smoking cubicle.

Stella waited for Jansen, who was on the phone once again. Seething with impatience, she stared at him until he finished the call.

"The case file. Can you tell me where it is?"

"It's there. On the table."

Jansen gave her an apologetic glance, and a small shake of his head, which spoke volumes to Stella. She knew that Grover's subordinate wasn't able to speak up against him, but she could tell from his facial expression that he was not happy with his boss's decision and that he didn't agree or approve.

But there was nothing he could do, and Stella could see that in this situation, Jansen had no option but to toe the line.

"I'm sorry about this," Jansen muttered, as he opened the folder. "Believe me, I strongly pushed for permission to join you on this case, but my suggestion was shot down. Grover is still angry with me for calling you in the first place."

"It's no problem," Stella muttered back, opening the suspiciously slim file.

The scanty paperwork included witness reports from Clint and his three friends who had arrived on the scene. They had not identified who'd first found the body, but Stella acknowledged this was not relevant. The killer would not have hung around for hours, to shout and scream with shock the next morning before running away. Most likely, Stella guessed some partygoers had been looking for a place to clean up before leaving, given the fact that the rest of the house was a disaster and the other bathrooms basically unusable.

There were no other witness reports, only short statements from both Clint's parents that they had been away, and their son had known nothing about the murder and had not been involved.

And there were no call records. Now feeling furious, Stella realized that Maxwell's request had been ignored.

"I can't believe this," Maxwell said, sounding livid.

Stella's suspicions were starting to crystallize. She had a feeling that Grover, who was presumably well connected and friendly with the parents in the area, wanted to protect these local youngsters, so that they would have a bright future unmarred by any charges or criminal record. She suspected he would not have the same accommodating attitude toward foreign students but that there was no way of discriminating between the two groups in the circumstances that had occurred at the party.

She wondered if one or more of the parents had pressured him to do this, and if so, whether any incentive had been offered.

"We'll have to call New Haven," Stella said. The office was very noisy, with at least three conversations taking place. "They can get hold of the cell company and prioritize the request. I'll go outside and do that. What's Desiree's phone number?"

With the information she needed, Stella headed out. After the overly warm office, outside was fresh and cool. She wished she could move the desk out here, and work in an area away from the oppressive environment of the back office.

Quickly, she called New Haven.

"I need help with accessing call and message records for a case under Special Agent Roth," she said.

"Hold the line," the receptionist said.

A moment later, a sharp and all-too-familiar voice crackled down the line.

"Agent Carrie Potts. How can I help?"

Stella closed her eyes for a moment. Not only were they being blocked by Grover, but she was now being forced to deal with her rival, Carrie Potts, who would do her utmost to sabotage Stella in any way she could.

It was only twenty past nine, and already, the day was turning into a disaster.

CHAPTER SIXTEEN

Things simply could not get any worse, Stella thought, feeling desperate. She wished she'd asked Maxwell to make the call to get Desiree's phone records. He would have had a better chance of a successful outcome.

For a moment she wondered if she should just hang up and ask him to try. Then she caught herself. That would be admitting defeat. She had to fight. And, after all, the last time they'd had a real conversation, she'd called Carrie out on her atrocious behavior. Since then, they'd been avoiding each other.

"It's Stella Fall here," she said.

"Oh," Carrie said, her voice now resonating with aggression. "What do you want?"

"I need help with call records," Stella said.

"You do?" Carrie sighed. "Why can't you pull them yourself?"

"Because I'm not in the office," Stella explained patiently. "The detectives at the local precinct, who should have requested them yesterday, are chasing another case and didn't help us. We need them urgently."

"What a pity you don't work well with others," Carrie muttered under her breath, the barbed words stinging Stella viciously.

"Believe me, we've tried," she said, her own anger and desperation audible in her voice, even though she knew it would only fuel Carrie to further vindictiveness.

"Which cell number? I'm quite busy this morning, helping with the money laundering case. But I'll try to do it when I have time," Carrie said.

Stella's heart accelerated to warp speed. They couldn't afford further delay.

"We can't move forward until we have them," she pleaded. "It's the Desiree Jardine murder case. Here's her number."

She was about to read it out, but was interrupted by Carrie's startled, "What?"

"Desiree Jardine," Stella repeated.

"Jardine? You're handling that?" Carrie sounded incredulous.

"Yes, it's one of Roth's new cases, as of yesterday," Stella said.

There was a pause.

"My mother knew her," Carrie said, and now she sounded different. The twang of enmity had disappeared from her voice. "She was Desiree's teacher, the whole way through primary school. They stayed friends afterwards. My mother's really upset about it."

"I'm so sorry to hear that," Stella said.

Carrie sighed. "Give me the number."

Stella read it out.

"I'll get the records for you immediately. I've dealt with this cell company before. I know exactly who to speak to, and they're quick." Carrie paused. Then she spoke again, with the anger back in her voice. "Why are you having problems with the local detectives? This case is too important for you to be starting your nonsense and creating political issues!"

"I'm not!" Stella practically shouted out the words, frustration boiling inside her. "The Putnam precinct has a dinosaur in charge, Detective Grover, who is furious that his assistant called us in. Grover is blocking us at every turn. He's convinced the case will go cold. He says there have been two similar cold cases in the past in his precinct. I'm sure he has personal reasons for not helping us. He's basically dumped us to work on our own. It's just me and Maxwell and so far, we've gotten nowhere on it. It's not our fault. We're having to walk on eggshells to stop this asshole from causing a full-scale department war!"

"Why is this happening?" Carrie shot back. "Are his personal reasons caused by your aggressive, antisocial behavior?"

"They are not! Without a doubt, Grover's incompetent. But, if you want my take on it, I suspect he's been bribed." The words burst from Stella's mouth. Too late, she clamped it shut. In her anger she'd said far too much.

Carrie was a local and might know Grover, or other people in his department. And Carrie was always on the lookout for ammunition to use against her. Stella had risen to her bait and had given her a ton of it. The comment she had just made was slanderous, and she had no proof to back it up apart from her own gut feeling. She could earn a disciplinary hearing, or even end up facing a defamation lawsuit, as a result of what she'd said.

"Interesting," Carrie said, and Stella didn't like the tone in her voice at all. She was sure Carrie was now well aware of the advantage Stella had given her. "I see. You'll have those records in a few minutes."

Abruptly, she disconnected.

Stella trailed back inside. She decided not to mention the confrontation she'd just had with Carrie. It would only demoralize Maxwell, too.

"The records should be emailed shortly," she explained.

"Okay. Let's set up," Maxwell said. He looked around the room. Where could they work?

There was only one unoccupied desk – unoccupied by people, at least. It was a small table in a corner that was piled with paperwork.

"I guess we go there," Stella said.

"Right you are," Maxwell replied.

Moving to the desk, she cleared enough space for them to work. They set out the meager contents of the file, opened up their laptops, and arranged the lists of names and the notes from yesterday.

Maxwell checked his mail. "The call log's just been sent through. That was very quick," he said, sounding relieved. "Shall we look for any red flags first, starting with the drug transaction?"

Stella was relieved, too, even though she knew that their advantage was likely to be temporary and that Carrie was plotting something diabolical in the longer term.

They set up their laptops with the call records open and scanned through the list of calls and texts.

Her first impression was that Desiree had spent a lot of time on her phone. She was clearly career focused. Checking the messages, Stella saw numerous work conversations. During working hours, she had made multiple calls, too. The nine-to-six pattern was obvious. Communication had been a key part of her job.

Outside of work hours, there were still a few work-related interactions, but the numbers of calls trailed off. There were social messages. Paging through, trying to get an overview, she noticed a few cheeky exchanges that were clearly sent to her lovers. Also, a few chats with her husband and son. These seemed to be short and friendly.

The problem was the sheer volume of communication, Stella decided. With only herself and Maxwell to handle this mass of information, it was going to be a sticking point that would slow them down.

"There's a ton of data here," Maxwell said, clearly thinking along the same lines in terms of the time this would take.

"I was wondering if we could speed it up somehow," Stella said.

"How would you do that?"

Maxwell stared at her across the desk, with one eyebrow quirked, and looking into his dark eyes, Stella felt a rush of warmth. The sensation was as unexpected as it was surprising. She remembered the clasp of his hand last night, his fingers linked in hers, and the way he'd gently stroked her hair as he put his arm around her.

Abruptly, she looked away.

She was starting to get emotionally entangled with him, she realized in shock. The spark between them wasn't going to disappear because they were discussing a case. Had she ever believed that work and romantic life could separate cleanly?

Quickly, she continued.

"We need to think like her. I feel she was a recreational drug user. There are no signs to indicate she was addicted. Her work told us she didn't drink during the week, so why would she behave differently where drugs were concerned?"

"Agreed. I doubt she was habitual."

"She probably wanted drugs to have some fun for the party. Therefore, she would most likely have obtained them on Friday or Saturday. There'd be no need to get them before that time and she would have had no use for them. They'd be lying around in her house, and she wouldn't want that, with her son visiting regularly."

Maxwell nodded understanding. "Given that she was a workaholic I'd say we could narrow it further. Friday evening, after she left the office, or Saturday."

"Let's focus on that time. From Saturday evening, and working back from there?"

Stella scrutinized the records closely. What evidence could she find of Desiree having contacted a friend, or a dealer, who supplied hard drugs?

Apart from her FBI training, Stella had no personal experience of people doing this. She'd never moved in the circles of people who did cocaine. In her tough, poor Kansas neighborhood she was sure there had been other drugs available, and alcohol had certainly been misused, but not coke. And she'd known nobody at university who had used it. Her ex's family had used, but she hadn't known any of their dealers. She felt out of her depth here. She hoped Maxwell, who'd had direct experience in drugs cases, would be able to spot something she might miss.

Sure enough, as he perused the records, Maxwell's eyes narrowed. "Look. Saturday afternoon. There's something weird here."

Maxwell turned his screen to Stella. "See this."

It was a message exchange.

Desiree had texted an unsaved number a single digit: 8.

The number had replied back with: 180.

Desiree had given a thumbs up, and the unknown number had replied with an address, which looked to be nothing more than a street corner.

"That's a drugs deal," Maxwell said. "The number 8 would be an eighth of a gram. From then on, it was price and location."

"Seriously?" Stella stared at the exchange, fascinated by her first real life evidence of a drugs transaction taking place. So this was what it looked like?

The problem was that this exchange seemed very unemotional. Business had been done. There was no indication that it was anything other than a fleeting moment where money had been exchanged for drugs. There seemed to be nothing that had gone wrong.

Or was there?

Stella's eyes narrowed as she read on. There was another exchange between them, a couple of hours later.

The unknown number had texted: *U screwed me. Needed 2 sell more. Tell me where ur going?*

Desiree had texted back: *FU. Not buying from u again.*

The unknown number had then angrily replied: *FU. I will find u.*

Desiree had texted a rude sign back and there had been no more interaction between them.

Stella's heart accelerated as she read through these increasingly angry messages. It was clear that the dealer had wanted more from her. Either he'd wanted her to buy more, or for her to give him the opportunity to sell more. Perhaps she'd told the dealer about the party but refused to say where it was. No doubt, she hadn't wanted to be followed there by a dealer in hard drugs. But perhaps she had been. He could have arrived there, angry, and things had then gone wrong.

"We need to find this guy," she said.

"Agreed," Maxwell's face was intent as he scanned the messages.

"Can we track the phone number?" she asked.

Maxwell shook his head. "We can try, but if it's a dealer's number, I doubt it will be linked to any GPS. They use older, burner phones. It won't give you more than a basic location." He tapped his fingers on the table thoughtfully. "We'll need to set up a deal. That will be the best way to find him. To meet in person and pretend to be a buyer."

"Shall we try now?"

"Yeah. Sooner the better."

Before she could think too hard about it, Stella took out her phone and texted the number 8 to the same number. She waited. They both peered down at the phone as the seconds ticked by.

"Nothing," she said, feeling disappointed.

And then it pinged with an incoming message. The number 180.

The dealer had taken the bait. Stella felt on edge with excitement and nerves.

Her hands were shaking as she messaged a thumbs-up back and waited for the address she hoped would follow.

Her phone pinged again, and she stared down.

Just like Desiree's message, this was nothing more than the name of two cross streets. It was north of downtown New Haven, and from Putnam, it would take them nearly an hour to get there.

"I'd better tell him a time," Stella said. As soon as possible would be best. She didn't want him to back out of the deal, and they were under pressure to solve this.

She texted back: 11 am?

The reply was a thumbs up.

The trap was set. For the sting to be successful, they would need to come face to face with the dealer. There was only one problem. Maxwell with his clean-cut appearance and cropped dark hair, looked far too much like law enforcement.

"I'll do it," Stella said.

CHAPTER SEVENTEEN

Stella parked the unmarked in a small strip mall a block away from the street corner. She didn't want the dealer to see it, as its police car type might ring alarm bells. A woman buying cocaine would be more likely to arrive in a fancier vehicle, she thought, as she climbed out and walked swiftly along the sidewalk. Nerves fizzed inside her. Maxwell had said he would wait nearby and out of sight, but she felt very alone as she headed to the rendezvous point.

She'd changed her top and was wearing a down jacket with a fake-fur collar that she hoped would look less like law enforcement than the navy coat she'd had on earlier.

Before they left the New Haven FBI headquarters, she'd removed her firearm and locked it away in Roth's safe. She didn't want the dealer to spot a gun holster. Even a glimpse of a concealed one might ring alarm bells, and he would surely be on the lookout for such clues.

She'd taken her hair out of its braid, and it swung over her shoulders. She hoped she looked like a normal customer. She hoped that this dealer would take the bait and wouldn't be somehow warned off when he saw her. They couldn't afford to fail.

As she waited, Stella glanced around, and drew in a sharp breath as she saw the black SUV again. It was the same car. The dent on the hood clued her in. It was parked near the street corner.

The driver must have followed her, staying a few cars back, because she'd been aware of the vehicles directly behind, but not this one.

Was this something to do with the case? If so, why wasn't Maxwell also being followed?

Stella had the feeling this was nothing to do with the case, but rather something more personal.

Dread swelled inside her. What did this guy want?

Stella remembered her promise to herself to confront him. Now was not a good time, in the throes of a sting operation, but she had to try. She turned and walked quickly in the direction of the car, but with a roar, it accelerated away.

Letting out a shaky breath, Stella turned back – to find a man waiting behind her.

This was him. It must be. He looked jumpy and wired. His skin was dull, his eyes hidden behind dark shades. He wore a baseball cap pulled down low over his ragged hair. The frayed sleeves of his jacket had ridden up, exposing arms that were blurrily inked.

How would a drug buyer react in this first-time encounter? She guessed her nervousness was reasonable enough.

"Hi," she said, giving him a wary nod.

He looked her up and down. She hoped that nothing about her signaled to his radar who she really was.

Even so, he seemed suspicious.

"Where'd you get my number?" he challenged.

It was time to set out the bait and see if this unknown, nameless man had played a part in Desiree's death.

"A friend of mine," Stella said, sounding cagey. "Name of Desiree."

"Desiree?"

"Slim, blond woman. She lives in Hartford. She said she bought from you recently?"

He nodded. "Okay."

His expression – what she could see of it – didn't change. He didn't show any signs of knowing about the murder, but as a dealer in hard drugs, he was no stranger to crime. He wasn't going to show the same level of unguarded reaction as the others she'd questioned.

"You got the money?" he asked.

"Sure." Stella reached into her purse, took out her wallet, fumbled through it, and showed him the sheaf of four fifty-dollar bills she'd drawn on the way. She needed to open a conversation with him before letting him touch the cash. How could she start? How could she steer the topic where it needed to go?

"I'm a bit nervous," she said. "I'm worried about getting sick from this. Is it pure?"

"I only sell pure," he said. He didn't look happy to be questioned.

"Do you sell to Desiree often?" she asked.

He shrugged. "Now and then."

He glanced over his shoulder as a man in running gear sped past. He was scrutinizing the cars, his radar clearly on high alert. She didn't know where Maxwell was.

She felt on edge, because she was picking up a lot of tension in this dealer. He was suspicious, jumpy. She suspected he was high at that moment or coming down from a high. Aggression simmered close to his surface. This guy was unpredictable and probably wouldn't hesitate to start a fight. There wasn't going to be much chance to question him, but she had to try.

"When's the last time you sold to her?" Stella asked.

His eyes narrowed. "Saturday," he said.

She still couldn't tell how much he knew.

"Did you sell her the same amount?"

"Yeah."

"Do you know what she needed it for? As I haven't been able to get hold of her since then. I'm worried about the quality," Stella said again, deciding this was the only line of conversation that might get her a step or two further.

"She said she was going to a party."

"You know where it was?"

"How would I know?" he said angrily, but Stella picked up the first signs of defensive body language. His left arm crossed protectively over his body. He was physically showing he wanted to block any further questions. His face was glowering and his mouth tight. His fingers were clenched. He was closing up. Had her question touched a nerve?

"She didn't tell you?" Stella asked.

"Why would she?" he snapped back.

Feeling as if she was walking an unsteady tightrope, Stella pressed on.

"I think she told you. I mean, you might have wanted to sell to other people, right? Wouldn't you have asked?"

Her accurate guess had triggered him. This man had now tipped over all the way into hard suspicion.

"Why d'you want to know this?"

"I'm a first-time buyer from you. I have concerns," Stella tried.

"Nobody has concerns, the way you're talking. Not Desiree the first time she bought, not anybody. There's no reason, lady. Not when people want good drugs."

"I was just asking," Stella protested.

"Nobody just asks," he snarled.

"Why won't you tell me? Do you know something about her?"

His arms twitched and she sensed that in the moment, he'd been about to lash out physically. Violence was his default reaction.

"I don't trust you. And I'm not doing business with you," he continued. His anger was surging. There was no way of redeeming the situation, Stella realized, as he snapped out, "Deal's off."

He turned and stalked away, ignoring her shouted plea of, "Wait!"

She'd blown it. Or perhaps, it had never been a possibility to get any information from this paranoid, aggressive man. Stella didn't think things could get any worse, but in a heartbeat they did.

Maxwell jumped out from behind a parked SUV nearby, where he'd been waiting out of sight. He ran toward the dealer.

"FBI! Stop!" he shouted.

Fear boiled inside her. This man was too wired, too on edge, to cope with this sudden surprise. This spelled disaster. Catastrophe.

She sprinted after the dealer, desperation fueling her speed. Without a weapon, she would have to physically prevent whatever might happen.

Even as she had the thought, the dealer thrust his hand into the pocket of his worn, shapeless jacket. Stella shouted in panic as he took out a gun.

Maxwell's hand locked onto his holster. He was drawing his Glock, but his actions were too late, he hadn't known or anticipated how keyed up this criminal was. Stella had known, and she hadn't done enough. She hadn't warned him and now this man was going to shoot. He was going to fire his gun before Maxwell, she could see the intent in every line of his body.

Stella couldn't bear to visualize what the consequences might be of a shot fired in anger, at such close range. It would be her fault if Maxwell was seriously injured or killed.

The dealer's hand jerked upward, grasping the gun. From pointing down at the floor, its barrel swung toward Maxwell's chest.

There was no time to think any more, but she was close enough now to act.

Stella leaped from behind and launched herself at the dealer. She grabbed him around his skinny waist and clung on for all she was worth. They crashed down onto the paving at exactly the same moment the gunshot exploded in Stella's ears.

Maxwell. Was he okay? Had he been hit?

There wasn't time to look. Gravel seared her cheek. The harsh reek of gunpowder filled her nostrils as she latched onto her target, fighting the struggling man for all she was worth. There was his weapon on the sidewalk. He'd dropped it as he fell.

Don't let him use it again, she thought. She managed to knock it out of his reach with her foot as he writhed around, trying to attack her. He was yelling, screaming. His face was grazed from the fall. Spittle showered her face, and the sour reek of his breath filled her nostrils.

Stella flung out her forearms to ward off the frenzy of his clawing blows. She managed to grab one of his arms, but he was crazily, impossibly strong and he wrenched it away from her.

With a power she didn't know she possessed, she grabbed his arm again, and this time clung on. Adrenaline sang through her veins. Her muscles were screaming as she held him back. His jabbing fingers were aiming for her eyes, but she had him, she was strong enough to stop him for now. She had to contain his attack and subdue him for long enough so that she could see if her partner was injured.

And then, he was wrenched away from her. With brutal force, Maxwell yanked him to his feet, twisting one of his arms up behind him so that he squealed in pain.

He hadn't been shot. He didn't look hurt. The bullet must have gone wide, or too low. Buoyed by relief, Stella leaped to her feet. She grabbed the dealer's skinny biceps, holding on tight as Maxwell fought to handcuff the now shrieking man.

Finally, she heard the click of the cuffs. As if a string had been snapped, the fight went out of him.

Stella felt battered and bruised. Her arms ached, her face stung, and she could still smell the stink of the dealer's breath and his greasy hair. She could barely make sense of the savage encounter that had just played out. Things had spiraled way out of control, and it brought home to her all the dangers of her job. A situation could go bad in a heartbeat when you were dealing with the dark side of society.

She'd tackled the dealer just in time, and had been able to save Maxwell's life, and now that the crisis was over, she was shaking all over with reaction and relief.

A few bystanders had gathered, watching in concern from a safe distance. One of them must have called the cops, because at that moment, sirens wailed as a vehicle from the local New Haven police station pulled up. Two uniformed officers jumped out and rushed over to help. In a moment, the dealer had been escorted to the back of the van.

They had a violent criminal in custody. Now, they could find out if he had murdered Desiree Jardine.

CHAPTER EIGHTEEN

After the slack, unhelpful attitude at Putnam under Detective Grover, the focus and energy of the New Haven cops was doubly impressive to Stella. By the time she and Maxwell arrived at the local police precinct, the cops had radioed them to say the dealer had been ID'ed, booked into custody, and was already in an interview room.

Maxwell parked his car and got out. His hands were still trembling, a fact Stella noted with amazement. She'd never seen Maxwell lose his cool before. She guessed having come so close to being shot had unnerved him deeply.

She knew for sure it had frightened her. She still felt lightheaded with adrenaline. This had brought home to her exactly how unpredictable their job could be. A sting operation could turn deadly in a nanosecond.

She didn't want to think what would have happened if she'd been a moment slower, if that bullet had hit Maxwell instead of plowing its way harmlessly into the sidewalk.

Her mind flashed back once again to her father's disappearance. With a renewed awareness that peril could lurk at every turn, Stella wondered again about Maxwell's suggestion that he might have been involved in a dangerous case at the time.

Before they headed into the police station, Maxwell stood for a moment, breathing deeply. Then he turned to her.

"Thanks for what you did," he said, quietly, but in heartfelt tones. It was all he needed to say. Stella nodded, feeling a powerful rush of emotion that briefly robbed her of words.

Then they walked briskly to the entrance of the New Haven Police Department.

The arresting officer was waiting for them in the front office.

"Your suspect is Joe Gibson. He's a repeat offender. A meth addict," he explained.

That accounted for the twitchiness, the edginess and paranoia, Stella thought as the officer continued. "He's been jailed in the past for assault, and for drug dealing. He had ten grams of cocaine on his person at this time."

Stella could see the person Joe was. Small-time, vicious, unpredictable. He didn't care if he went into prison for six months or six years. Meth might have fried his brain badly enough for him not to be able to reason in a crisis.

His record would be a sticking point, because he had no incentive to tell them anything. He was their worst nightmare, a seasoned criminal who already knew that significant jail time awaited him.

There was only one way to deal with this, Stella decided, as the arresting officer led the way to the interview room. They were going to have to come down on him hard, with the attitude he was already guilty of Desiree's murder. If they could convince him they were serious enough, he would then be forced to argue his side, and somewhere between the two opposing versions, the truth might emerge.

"You've got to get him scared," she murmured to Maxwell. "Tell him he did it and make him fight back."

Maxwell nodded in agreement as the arresting officer opened the door.

"All yours," he said, as they walked into the small, brightly lit room.

Joe stared at them defiantly from the far side of the table. His hands were cuffed behind him, but his legs were shifting restlessly. His body was twitching as if bugs were crawling under his shirt, and she thought he must be on his way down from whatever he was on.

Maybe in a few hours, reality and rock bottom would hit with a thump. He'd be more vulnerable then, but they needed answers now.

Maxwell walked up to Joe, looming over him threateningly.

"You're in big trouble," he said to Joe. "Big trouble."

"For what?" Joe questioned defiantly. "Drawing a gun? You were about to assault me! I'm entitled to defend myself. I didn't shoot it. That woman pushed me from behind. That's the only reason it fired. Accidental discharge." His gaze flickered to Stella.

Maxwell sneered. "You think we're worried about that? It's Saturday you should be worrying about. What happened on Saturday will land you in jail for life."

Joe stared at him. For the first time, he seemed unsure.

"You got the wrong guy," he said.

"That's strange. I would say we have the right one. At any rate, your description ties in with some of the witness reports," Maxwell bluffed.

Stella decided to come in with a softer approach. Fear alone might not be enough of an incentive for Joe to crumble under Maxwell's dire threats. She wanted to provide another doorway for him to volunteer the information more willingly

Two options were better than one, especially since she didn't yet understand his personality, or whether he might shut down completely when attacked.

"Maxwell, let's hear his side, and allow him to speak for himself," she reasoned.

"Hear his side after he tried to kill me?" Maxwell shot back, pressuring Joe hard with his forceful point of view. "He's a murderer. He's proved it. All we have to do is make sure he gets life for what he did to her."

"Wait! Just wait a minute. Are you saying that woman, Desiree, is dead?" Joe asked, sounding incredulous.

"Such a surprise to you?" Maxwell jeered. "Such a surprise that you know who we're talking about straight away?"

Stella turned to Joe, her face serious. "Yes, she is dead. That's why we pulled her calls and messages. We read your messages and saw the deal you made to sell to her."

"There's no proof I actually sold anything to her," Joe argued.

"It appears you did. After the sale, there were other messages. Can you explain those?" Stella asked.

"I – I don't even remember the messages," Joe stammered. "I text people all the time. Say tons of stuff. Don't mean half of it."

"You were threatening her!" Maxwell said.

Stella saw the blank expression on the drug dealer's face and the tension in his shoulders. Joe was shutting down. The hard approach had reached its limits for the moment, and it was time to reason with him again.

"We can show the messages to you, and you can explain. Perhaps Desiree didn't buy as much as you hoped?" Stella suggested to Joe.

Quickly, Maxwell left the room and returned with the printed transcript.

He passed it to Joe, who read slowly through. As he reached the end of the conversation, his face tightened. That shifty look was back. He knew he was in bad trouble, Stella thought.

"Yeah. She didn't buy a lot. I wanted her to take more. I knew she had the money," Joe admitted grudgingly. "But nothing else happened. I swear it."

"Did you know she was going to a party?" Stella asked.

"She might have mentioned it," Joe admitted cagily.

"Did you ask her where it was?"

"She didn't say." Joe looked down at the desk's well-scrubbed plastic surface.

"I think you did more than ask her, Joe," Stella theorized. "You must have been disappointed that's all she bought. She's not a big customer. And going into winter, with the colder weather, is less of the party season. You needed the money. You pestered her to take you to the venue. Perhaps you lost your temper."

"You're wrong," Joe shot back, a reflexive response.

"I don't think she's wrong," Maxwell said in a hard voice. "I think you're hungry. Business hasn't been good. And you have a bad temper. Your messages to Desiree prove it."

"I do, but so what?" he retaliated.

"You were quick to say our deal was off," Stella explained. "You act impulsively. You got into an argument. Perhaps you didn't want to accept that she was rude to you and said she wouldn't buy from you again?" Stella was feeling her way, but she saw his face change and knew she was on the right track.

"Yeah. Yeah. I tried to argue back, as the messages show. But then I dropped the subject. I wasn't going to waste any more time on her."

Stella shook her head. "You felt she owed you. I don't think you would have left it. I think you followed her. You tracked her – the address where you met up is close to her house. You drove behind her when she went out later."

She watched him carefully. She was making up a story for him, but it was plausible. What would his reaction be?

"I did not!" he said.

"What part of my theory don't you agree with?" Stella pushed.

"All of it!" he retaliated.

"Your words are telling me one thing, but your face is telling me another. The way you're shifting your feet is a reveal. How you turned your head when I said you tracked her is a tell. I'm wondering, if we asked some of the people at the party, whether they would remember you? Because you're a little older than most of the guys who were there, and you look quite distinctive. I think they might recognize you."

Joe sighed. "Stop reading my mind," he said grumpily.

"Tell the truth, and I won't have to interpret what you really mean," Stella responded.

"Okay. You got me. When we met up, she did say the party was in Putnam. So I took a chance. I came back later and waited by the main road until I saw her car, and then I tried to track her there. But it wasn't because I was angry at her, I swear. I wanted to find new customers. I wanted to make more sales. She's a wealthy woman, she drives the latest Merc. I hoped she'd have rich friends. I followed her but I lost her along the way, took a wrong turn. It took me a while to find the place. It was in the middle of nowhere."

"What time was that?" Stella asked.

"I don't know. After midnight, I'd say. Perhaps an hour or two after. Eventually I followed a cab that ended up there. I went in, but it wasn't like I thought it would be. I couldn't see her there, and there were these two frat guys at the door who looked like bouncers. I said I'd come to find her, and they got mad. They basically chased me off. I left. I swear I did. I went straight home."

He rubbed his bicep, as if remembering how he'd been mishandled.

Stella glanced at Maxwell, who was looking as purposeful as she felt. Someone as sneaky, desperate and aggressive as Joe would surely not have given up. The more he was prevented from finding Desiree, the hungrier for revenge he might have become.

He'd lied throughout the interview, and she didn't trust him now. Wherever he had gone next, Stella was certain it hadn't been straight home. Had Joe crept around the house to find another way in, or doubled back after he'd been chased off?

Someone from the party must know. Someone must have seen. Tracking Joe's movements was now a matter of urgency.

CHAPTER NINETEEN

Stella decided the best starting point to find out more about the fight would be Clint. He might know which of his friends had been caught up in the brawl by the front door. She stepped out of the interview room and dialed his number, hoping he'd pick up fast when he saw who was calling.

Clint answered with apprehension in his voice. "Hello, agent?"

"I need more information from you, please. We believe an uninvited guest showed up at about one in the morning, and some guys at your party chased him off. Do you know anything about that, or who those guys would be?"

Clint paused. Then he replied, sounding thoughtful.

"Jaikaar and Palvinder were involved, for sure. Someone told me that they'd fought off some bad elements before they left. I didn't know what they meant. Or who else was with them, as I didn't see them leave. But they're on the list I gave you and both in residence at the university."

Stella thanked him and hung up, immediately dialing the first of the two numbers. Jaikaar didn't answer, but Palvinder, the second number she tried, picked up.

"It's FBI Agent Fall on the line. I need to ask you and Jaikaar some questions about Saturday," Stella said.

"FBI?" Palvinder repeated, sounding alarmed.

"Correct," Stella explained.

"I've just finished class, ma'am. Jaikaar will be available in half an hour. We can meet you at the campus coffee shop, if you like?"

He spoke in strongly accented, but excellent English.

"Sounds good," Stella said. "See you in half an hour."

She headed through to the front office. Maxwell had left the interview room while she was on the phone and was waiting with the cops who were ready to process Joe's arrest.

"Joe went to the party. He arrived sometime after one, but he said he never found Desiree and that he was run off at the door. I've found two witnesses who Clint thinks were involved. I'm going to go and speak to them now and see if they know whether Joe really left."

“I’ll wait here,” Maxwell said with a glance at the other cops. “If you find out any new information, I can double check it this side.”

“That sounds like a good plan,” Stella agreed.

Heading out of the New Haven police department, she set off for the University of Connecticut. As she drove, she realized this would be her first time back on a campus since she’d graduated with her master’s degree in forensic psychology from the University of Chicago.

Thinking back, Stella felt surprised all over again that even though she’d chosen to pursue a degree that was relevant to a law enforcement career, she hadn’t considered that direction at the time. Not after what had happened to her father, and her mother’s dire threats and warnings. She’d always imagined she would end up working in the legal field.

And now, here she was, in a career she never dreamed she would pursue, in charge of her first-ever solo case, and following up on a promising lead. If this interview went well, she might obtain the proof they needed to convict Joe Gibson of the crime.

*

When Stella hurried into the coffee shop, she saw it was quiet, with some students rushing in to purchase to-go cups, but not many seated. She saw the dark-haired Jaikaar and Palvinder immediately. They were seated together, talking in a language that Stella guessed was Punjabi. They looked like brothers, or perhaps even twins.

The closer of the two leaped to his feet when he saw her. Immediately, Stella realized how effectively he could have run off the scrawny Joe. He was well over six feet tall, fit and strong looking. No wonder Joe had described the two as bouncers.

“Hi. I’m Palvinder Khan,” he said.

“And I’m Jaikaar Khan.” Confirming Stella’s thoughts that they were related, the other man scrambled to his feet.

“You are Agent Fall, right?” Palvinder regarded her with what she guessed was admiration.

“Yes. Please, sit,” Stella said. “Can I buy you a drink?”

“Hot chocolate would be great,” Palvinder said, with a glance at Jaikaar, who nodded.

Quickly, Stella detoured to the counter and picked up three large hot chocolates. She returned to the table, and they all sat down.

“Tell me about the party, and how the evening played out,” Stella said.

Her first impressions of Jaikaar and Palvinder were that they didn't seem guilty, or worried about the consequences of the party. This was confirmed by Palvinder, who placed his elbows on the small cafeteria table and leaned toward her earnestly.

"It was a very wild night," he admitted. "We were invited by Clint, but there were a lot of gatecrashers there, including a few non-students, or at any rate, people who I've never seen at U-Conn. They drank very heavily and started a lot of trouble, and then some of the younger guys joined in."

"Do you remember a fight taking place outside at any stage?" Stella asked.

"The fight. Well, it wasn't really a fight," Palvinder explained. "It was more of a removal." He gave her a flashing, confident grin.

"Explain?" Stella said.

"It was at about half past one in the morning, and it occurred because we were getting rid of a few drunk guys who'd been having a massive game throwing plates across the lounge. My brother and I decided we had to get them off the premises, as they were destroying the house." Palvinder regarded her with quiet pride.

"How did you get rid of them?" Stella asked.

"We escorted them out, and then called a cab for them," Jaikaar stated, with all the assurance of somebody who was six-foot-three and comprised of two-hundred pounds of mostly muscle.

"Did anyone else arrive at that time?" Stella asked.

"In fact, yes. We were outside, watching the cab depart, when this old car pulled up," Palvinder said.

"We could see straight away it was trouble. I mean, he looked like a problem guy. He was much older than everyone else. Definitely in his late thirties, I would say."

"He was scruffy looking, and the car was an old jalopy," Palvinder confirmed.

"So yes, we thought he was trouble, and from the look of him, we immediately suspected he could be a drug dealer. Our first idea was that someone from the party had called him to come along. We decided we needed to manage the situation. We couldn't do anything about all the drinking, but we could definitely stop this unwanted guy from coming in and causing further problems."

"So you did that?" Stella asked.

"Yes. He walked up to the front door, very aggressive looking, and asked where Desiree was. He said he was here for Desiree and that she'd invited him."

"Did you know who Desiree was?" Stella asked.

"Yes. Yes, we did know who she was," Jaikaar exchanged a glance with Palvinder. "We noticed her arrive earlier. We had seen her at parties before," he hesitated.

"She had a reputation. We knew that already, from a friend of ours," Palvinder added.

"That's so," Jaikaar confirmed.

"Where was Desiree at the time?" Stella asked. One-thirty a.m. was approaching the window of time in which she had been murdered.

"At that time, most of the remaining guests were dancing in the hall. I didn't see her there, though," Palvinder said. "I remember looking back into the hall when he asked for her. Because she was not there, it meant this unsavory character would go roaming through the house to find her. That was what I thought."

He drained his hot chocolate and stared out of the cafeteria window thoughtfully, as if piecing together what he remembered of the night.

"How did you stop him from coming in?" Stella asked.

"When we asked him to leave, he became argumentative," Palvinder said. "We were not in the mood for arguing by then," he said.

"I was ready to go home," Jaikaar said.

"He started shouting and wanting to force his way in, so we told him there was no point in doing that, and that Desiree had left," Palvinder said.

"Okay," Stella said, deciding that was clever. "And he believed you?"

"No. He kept insisting that we were lying, that he'd seen her Mercedes outside and he wanted to look for her, so we decided we would put him back in his car," Palvinder smiled. "We took his arms and walked him down the driveway to his car. We told him that if he did not drive away, we would call the police and that they might want to search him and his car. Like I said, we wanted to leave by then, and did not have time for this man."

"And did he seem convinced by that?"

Palvinder nodded. "He seemed worried. He did not want the police to search his car, that was for sure, which confirmed our idea that he was a dealer of some kind. He got into his car, and he departed, fast."

"Did you warn Desiree about him?" Stella asked.

"No. Like I said, we were not sure where she was, or – or what she might be doing." Palvinder looked uneasy. "We called a cab and left shortly afterward. We did see him again while we were on the main road driving back."

"You did?"

"His car was very easy to recognize. It had a big dent in the rear bumper. We both noticed it. He was driving much more slowly, and as we watched, he turned in the direction of a nightclub just off the main road."

"So you think he was heading there?"

Palvinder nodded. "The nightclub is well known. Notorious, in fact. It's called King of Clubs, and it's in an industrial zone on the outskirts of New Haven. We assumed he was going there to do some business."

Stella nodded.

"That's important information. Give me a sec while I send a message."

A nightclub in an industrial zone might well have camera surveillance on the premises or in the surrounding area. If so, they could check the footage and see exactly when Joe had arrived, and more importantly, when he left again. If he had left the club during the time she'd been murdered, and gone back in the direction of Putnam, it would be highly suspicious.

She messaged the details to Maxwell, asking him to investigate the footage, and look up the dealer's plates.

Although Stella was grateful for this information, she felt worried that their lead was no longer looking as good as she had hoped. Until Maxwell could confirm whether Joe had left King of Clubs, or stayed there the rest of the night, Stella knew she'd have to keep moving forward.

There were still more questions to ask the brothers while she was here. She needed to probe deeper into the mention of Desiree.

"Tell me about Desiree's reputation. You said you heard about it from your friend?" she asked, putting her phone away.

"It was as a result of something that took place a while ago," Palvinder circled his spoon slowly through his chocolate, swirling it through the foam.

"A year and a half ago. In April or May. Definitely before the summer break," Jaikaar said.

"Wait a minute," Stella needed to clarify this. "You're saying that a year and a half ago, something happened?"

Jaikaar nodded. “Yes. She had an affair with one of our friends.”

“A year and a half ago?” Stella repeated.

Jaikaar and Palvinder exchanged a glance.

“It was just before the summer break,” Palvinder confirmed.

This was a bombshell. If this was true, it meant that Desiree had been cheating on her husband long before they were divorced.

“Did she attend student parties back then?” Stella asked, wanting to get a better handle on how, exactly, this had occurred. Surely, she couldn’t have been practicing this party going behavior back then, as a married woman? People would surely have talked about it.

“No. I didn’t see her at any parties. I think she and Tom just – just got together. He was on the ice hockey, athletics, and basketball team that year. We were on the basketball team also. And she was involved in some way with our team.”

“The fashion company she worked for sponsored a championship prize, I remember. That’s how they met,” Jaikaar added.

Palvinder clicked his fingers. “Yes! That’s it. Now it’s coming back to me. They sat next to each other at the prize giving ceremony and talked up a storm. Then, they left together. We saw them leave and were extremely curious. Later, he told us that she had invited him to go on to a hotel for drinks.”

“And more,” Jaikaar elaborated. “Drinks and more. She booked a room and dropped him home after midnight.”

Palvinder nodded. “Yes. So that’s the first time we really knew about her. Definitely an unusual woman.”

“What did your friend Tom think of this? Did he want to take it further? Or did she?” Stella asked.

“No, no. Absolutely not. Tom was ashamed about it. Knowing that she was married and all. He didn’t feel good about it afterwards. He told us what had happened because we had seen, and because we asked.”

“It took some persuasion for him to admit to it,” Jaikaar added.

“Tom begged us not to tell anybody else, as he thought he had made a mistake. And that people could be angry with him. Her husband in particular,” Palvinder summarized. “He was worried that she might try to make it a regular thing with him. But she didn’t.”

“I think I might even have some of the messages still saved,” Jaikaar said thoughtfully. He took out his phone and began scrolling.

“Jaikaar never deletes his messages. He’s like a walking record of U-Conn,” Palvinder joked.

"Okay, here we go." Flipping back through the screens, Jaikaar showed Stella the old conversation.

"Tom, dude! What happened last night with that lady from the function? We saw you get into her car?"

"Tom? Are you awake?"

An hour later, the reply. *"I'm awake."*

"Well? What happened?"

"Nothing."

"Dude! You got into the car with her!"

"She gave me a ride home."

"We watched. You went the other way. Into town."

"Yeah, well. I'm not talking to you anymore. Not on text anyway."

"We'll be there now."

Stella nodded. Though she had not confirmed directly with Tom, this conversation was compelling evidence that the same pattern had taken place with him.

"Where is Tom now?" she wondered if he'd been at the party.

"He's at home. He fell last week in ice hockey practice, and broke his ankle. It required an operation, and he has to recover at home until next week, I think."

That crossed Tom off the suspect list. But this indicated that Desiree's behavior had been going on for much longer than she'd first believed.

Palvinder's observation had been very relevant. Finding out that his wife had cheated on him while married could, indeed, have made Desiree's husband angry.

Now, Stella wondered if she'd questioned Walter thoroughly enough during their earlier interview. If she'd known Desiree had been cheating for years while married, rather than months while divorced, her questions would have been different. Perhaps Walter's answers would have been different, too.

A cheating wife complicated the situation and provided a stronger motive for murder. Furious and humiliated, Walter could have bided his time and taken revenge.

If he hadn't known about the cheating, Walter might still have some information on Desiree's previous lovers. Perhaps he might remember if she'd 'hung out' with a certain guy for a while or mentioned someone's name repeatedly.

Desiree Jardine. Not just a woman who'd had affairs during a rebellious phase post-divorce, but a woman who'd been doing so for much longer.

While she waited for Maxwell to confirm Joe's alibi in more detail, Stella decided she was going to interview Walter again.

CHAPTER TWENTY

An hour and a half later, at twelve-thirty in the afternoon, Stella pulled up outside Walter Jardine's offices in Saratoga Springs. It had been a long drive. She had tried to suppress her growing anxiety as the miles and minutes passed, reassuring herself by thinking that this trip might lead to a breakthrough in the case.

Walter owned a clothing distribution company. When she arrived at the premises, Stella was surprised by the scale of it. Set in a commercial part of town, the modern, glassed, double-story offices backed onto an enormous warehouse.

She headed to the tall glass entrance door and hurried inside.

"Is Walter Jardine available?" she asked the receptionist.

The well-groomed woman, who looked to be in her mid-thirties, was fashionably dressed in a beautifully cut top and a jacket made from brightly printed fabric.

She looked at Stella, surprised.

"He's in meetings the entire day. Did you book some time with his PA?" she asked.

"He needs to make time," Stella said firmly. "I'm from the FBI. It's in connection with his ex-wife's murder."

Immediately the receptionist's eyes widened, and she nodded somberly.

"Oh, that's such a terrible situation. Yes, I'm sure he can make time. Let me organize it. Please, take a seat." She gestured to the red leather couches on the other side of the room.

Stella walked over to the couches and sat, feeling impatient. She hoped that she would be able to see Walter soon.

As she waited, her phone buzzed. It was Maxwell. Filled with anticipation, she read his message.

"Camera footage confirms that Joe was parked at King of Clubs until 4.30 a.m. He then left in the direction of New Haven," the message read. *"I questioned him about his movements after he left the party. After some evasion, he confirmed he was there."*

Stella pressed her lips together.

With Joe now finally ruled out as a suspect, this next interview was even more critical.

She jumped to her feet as the receptionist called out to her.

"Mr. Jardine is in the small boardroom. I'll take you there now."

Stella followed her up the stairs to the second floor. There, the receptionist opened the door, showing a room elegantly decked out with a round wooden table and six leather-upholstered office chairs.

Walter Jardine was alone in the room. He stood up when he saw Stella.

"Is there any news?" he asked anxiously.

"No news as yet," Stella said. "Please, sit."

Walter frowned, lowering himself heavily back onto his chair as she sat opposite.

"Why are you here, then?"

If he was guilty, he was hiding it skillfully. He was coming across as innocent, puzzled by her arrival.

"We've uncovered further information on the case. As a result, I need to reconfirm your alibi in more detail," Stella said politely. She watched him carefully as she spoke.

"What information?" Walter asked. When Stella didn't reply, he continued. "I – I was at home. I don't know what more I can tell you. I was on a conference call in the early evening. Peter had two friends over, and we ordered pizza at about seven. They spent most of the night in the family room, which I set up as a gaming room. I watched a movie and went to bed at about ten."

Stella noted that his son had been shut away in the family's lounge, gaming. Theoretically, Walter could have climbed in his car after midnight, arrived at the party at two a.m., murdered Desiree, and been home before four.

To do that, he would have needed a strong motive, and also to have known that Desiree would be at the party.

"Did you know where Desiree was that night?" Stella asked.

"No. There was no reason for me to think she was anywhere. She hadn't asked us to house sit so I assumed she was at home. I can show you our calls and messages if you want to see them. The last time we communicated was two weeks ago, when Peter visited her for the weekend. Is this all you came to ask? I've already explained that I have no motive whatsoever to murder my ex-wife. I wished her only well."

"Please show me your calls and messages," Stella said.

"Sure."

Stella waited while he scrolled through his phone.

"Here's the calls." He showed her. "Here's the messages."

Stella read through. The messages sounded formal, but friendly. The last one was a text from Desiree two weeks before the party saying, *"Pete enjoyed his weekend! Wish him luck for the exams. I'll be away for a few days in early December, and I'll be in touch before then."*

Desiree had last called him a few days before sending that message. Presumably, that had been to organize Peter's weekend.

"Thanks," Stella said.

It didn't seem likely that Walter had known about the party. And their last communications had been friendly. She was reassured he hadn't known where Desiree was on Saturday night, and she hadn't missed any nuances or information in the first round of questioning. This meant she had a tough task ahead. She had to tell the bereaved Walter what his wife had been doing behind his back.

She really didn't want to do this, but it was now essential for the case. In his innocence, Walter might have seen or heard something helpful. He might have observed Desiree speaking or interacting with the killer.

Tough as this was going to be, she had to find out.

"Unfortunately, there's something I have to explain to you. We've uncovered additional background on Desiree," Stella said. She felt a sense of regret as she said the words. "Mr. Jardine, your wife was having affairs. Multiple affairs, including with some of the students who were at the party."

Walter stared at her, surprise turning to incredulity.

"Affairs?" he asked.

"Were you aware of them?" Stella asked.

"I have no idea about her behavior or relationships after we divorced," Walter said, with the righteousness back in his voice again. "All I know was that she was not in a steady relationship. At any rate, she didn't tell me so. And I don't think her actions after the divorce could count as affairs in any case. We were both free to see other people if we chose."

"We're not only talking about after the divorce. We're also talking about during the marriage. In the past year or two. We have been told that she had at least one short affair during this time. Probably, more than one. Did you know about this?" Stella asked, clocking his reaction carefully.

Walter stared at her in shock. He looked as if he'd seen a ghost.

Was he shocked because she'd found out, or genuinely appalled at the bombshell that had landed? Stella wasn't sure which. She couldn't tell from his reaction. But now, while he was vulnerable and unsettled, was the time to push forward.

"Well? Mr. Jardine?" she hassled him.

"You're trying to trap me, aren't you?" he said, but his voice was unsteady now. "Why are you misleading me like this? Are you out of suspects, and needing to bring someone in?"

"No. We're not out of suspects. We are actively searching for suspects. We are focused on bringing in the correct person, with a motive for the murder," Stella said. "Even if you were unaware of what she was doing, you might still know something that could help us."

Walter shook his head. It seemed as if he was actually trying to shake off her words, his actions were so violent.

"That's not true. None of this is true!" he insisted angrily. "You're lying! She couldn't have been doing that."

His entire demeanor had changed, Stella saw. He was quivering with outrage. His face was twitching, his hands clenched.

"Were there no late nights?" Stella asked. "No events she attended on her own? Industry functions? Prize givings? Are you certain her goings and her doings were all work related?"

She stared at him sternly. She expected more defiance from him, but instead, she watched his angry expression crumble into despair.

"Do you want proof?" she added.

"No!" Walter cried. "Please, no. I'm sure you have it, but I don't want it. I can't believe this. I can't cope with this now."

Stella wasn't sensing any guilt from him. His reaction seemed genuine. He was now on the brink of tears. As if he'd had an image of his wife that was being shattered.

Even though she knew the affairs would have been made public if this case got as far as court, she felt terrible that she had been the one to tell him this.

"I can't imagine she would have done such a thing," Walter cupped his forehead in his hands, sounding agonized. "And yet, at the same time, I can. I can see her doing that. She was that person. We were so mismatched and yet, we loved each other. We tried so hard, but it didn't work. I think she was unhappy with me, and her unhappiness made her act recklessly. She rebelled."

He stared at Stella.

"I don't want to know what she did. Please don't tell me. Please don't bring me into the picture. I was not involved in her murder. And it's breaking me to have to confront this."

Stella's heart clenched as she realized Walter was blinking tears away.

She believed him. Even though his alibi did leave a small window of time where it might have been possible, she accepted that he hadn't spoken to Desiree for nearly two weeks and did not know she was at the party. And his reaction now seemed authentic.

She wished she could leave him in peace to process the shocking facts he'd just learned, but she had more questions to ask. Walter might still hold the key to the killer's identity.

"Who else could possibly have done this?" she questioned, more gently, after a pause. "Can you think of anyone at all who might have had a motive to murder your wife? Was there anyone she was angry with? Any conflict you noticed? Anyone she started talking about, or spending time with, when you were married?"

Walter shook his head helplessly.

"I can't recall anything like that. Unfortunately, we did end up leading quite separate lives. She did her thing; I did my thing. She went to a lot of work events, and I stopped going with her. I'm sure some of them weren't even work events but like I said, I don't want to know about that now."

"I understand," Stella said.

"Fashion's a young industry. She looked young and took care of herself. Invested in her appearance. She had a lot of younger friends. She was always out at parties and functions, although I don't know how she would have ended up at Clint Woods's party. It must be close to two years since we last saw them. One of Carolyn's birthday parties was the last event we were invited to."

"I hope you understand we needed to confirm this," Stella said gently.

"Absolutely," Walter's logical perspective, that she'd first sensed, was prevailing once again. His loss of balance had been temporary. "I appreciate that you are exploring every possibility. Believe me, if you lean on others the same way you have just leaned on me, I'll be glad. Anything I can do, however small, let me know. If I can help in any way at all, just call me." His face fell. "This has been a huge blow. But it's all the more reason to find the killer. Even if my wife made mistakes. Even if that happened. There's no reason she should have to die that way as a result." His voice shook with emotion, "No reason at all!"

Stella felt strangely touched by his words.

"Thank you for your help," she said.

"Whatever I can do, I will," he said quietly. "If you're done now, can you please leave? I need some time alone before I return to my other meeting."

She left him sitting in the boardroom, his head bowed.

Stella trailed out, feeling as if she had reached rock-bottom on this case. What if it did grow cold? What if the justice that Walter had just begged for, was never found?

Try as she might, she could think of no further directions to explore. Apart from one.

Perhaps the person who always gave her advice and support, in the darkest of hours, might be able to provide some insight.

CHAPTER TWENTY ONE

"Hello? Clem?" Stella felt relieved as she heard his voice on the line. In the early afternoon, her university mentor, who also happened to be a retired FBI agent, was often busy taking classes or giving lectures at the University of Chicago.

She'd waited until she'd arrived back at the New Haven police department before calling him, in case she needed to take notes while they spoke. Now, she was sitting in her car outside the precinct.

"Hey, Stella," Clem responded. "You caught me in between lectures. I'm walking through the university. It's a six-minute walk to the next hall. So we have six minutes to speak," he said, sounding pleased by the precision of the timing.

"I need your advice on a problem case," she said.

"You probably don't," Clem said, sounding amused, but also intrigued. "Most likely, you just think you do. But I'm always happy to discuss case theory, and for that, I can set aside as much time as you need, even if I call you back later. Tell me the problem."

"It's a murder case. Victim was forty years old, recently divorced, partying at a bash held by a university student. She was found with a cable tie around her neck. She died in the small hours of the morning. The party was wild, and everyone was very drunk."

"Go on?" Clem's voice had sharpened, and she knew he was already captivated by this mystery.

"We can't find anyone with a motive for doing it. Not the party host. None of the partygoers we've interviewed so far. She had a habit of sleeping with younger guys and then moving on, but most of them didn't mind, or have alibis for the time of death. Her ex-husband is cleared. The drug dealer she bought cocaine from, who arrived at the party to find her, is cleared."

"Interesting case," Clem said. "It seems like there's a lot more to her personality and circumstances than you would think at first."

"I feel I've been peeling back layers," Stella agreed.

"She doesn't seem to have been on a good path," Clem said.

"I think her behavior was escalating. Affairs, drugs, parties. I'm wondering if she started off rebelling against a loveless marriage that she considered boring, and then it snowballed to a point where she couldn't stop."

"Until someone stopped it for her," Clem finished.

"Exactly," Stella said.

"You're doing everything right," Clem reassured her. "I'm certain you'll get to the core of this case if you continue on this line of thinking."

"But how?" Stella pleaded. "We're out of suspects! We have a long guest list from the party host, with everyone he remembers being there, but interviewing people feels like playing a lottery and losing every time, because everyone was crazy drunk, and nobody there seems to have a strong motive for wanting her dead."

"No. You're not out of suspects at all. It just feels like it because you have ruled out the most obvious ones. But maybe, given the escalation you described, you should look at it from a different perspective."

"What do you mean by that?" Stella felt herself calming down. Clem's cool, methodical logic always had that effect. He always made her feel more centered, more capable. She wished she had his capacity to channel and discipline her thoughts.

"With those circumstances and the *modus operandi*, it seems preplanned, and unlikely to have been a crime of passion," he said.

"Yes," Stella agreed.

"Your line of investigation already shows me that you're looking into her history. That you've realized the motive for this murder must have existed before the party happened."

"That's correct," Stella said.

"Someone knew she was going to be there and planned it. Depending on how recently the party was organized, tells you how long they had to plan. So go back to that starting point. Check the date."

Stella nodded. When Clem put it like that, the timeline of preparation that the killer would have had, seemed more manageable.

"Now, since it was preplanned, perhaps that person never intended to be seen at the party at all," Clem continued.

Stella felt her skin prickle into gooseflesh. Clem's words had led her to the "A-ha" moment she needed.

"That's it!" she exclaimed. "I've been battling with the whole concept of the guest list, and you've shown me exactly why. Someone who preplanned a killing wouldn't have wanted to be seen there. They would have covered their tracks and created an alibi. So we've been ignoring the group of people that the killer was part of. And that's the group of people who weren't on the guest list."

"Exactly," Clem agreed, sounding as excited as Stella felt. "You need to look at who wasn't there. Who had a non-presence, rather than a presence at the party."

"I'm going to follow that direction immediately," Stella said. "I knew you'd help me think it through. You always do."

"You can do this, Stella. Have faith in your abilities. Keep focusing on the bigger picture and trust your intuition," Clem advised.

"Thank you," Stella said.

She disconnected feeling as if a whole new set of possibilities had opened up in her mind. That was the benefit of speaking to Clem. He had a way of asking exactly the right questions. Now, all Stella had to do was find the answers.

As she put her phone away, a familiar shape caught her eye. Sleek, black, shiny. Parked across the road, in the parking lot for the doctors' rooms opposite the police station. Gasping in disbelief, Stella noted the dent on the hood and the XD on the plate.

It was the black Lexus, here once more. This time, she was going to find out exactly who was following her. She was not going to let the driver speed away again.

The car was parked facing the low wall that separated the parking lot from the road. It couldn't leave the parking space by going forward and could only reverse out. So if she could get behind it in time, she would effectively trap the driver in place.

Filled with determination despite the possible dangers, Stella jumped out of her car and sprinted across the road as fast as she could. Speed was essential if she was going to catch him unawares.

She leaped over the low wall just as she heard the engine start up.

And then, she was behind the car. She'd done it, and he had been too slow. The car revved desperately, but she planted her feet in place. She'd been through too much in the past two days to be intimidated by a revving engine. If he thought that was going to make her move away, he was wrong.

"Get out of your vehicle," she shouted. She bashed the back window with the flat of her hand, hoping the noise would startle him and also serve as a subtle threat about what else she could do if he didn't decide to talk to her.

There was a pause. And then, slowly, the driver's door opened.

The open door seemed like an invitation, but even as Stella made the move toward it, she caught herself. She had to stay behind the car. He hadn't killed the engine. The moment she shifted away, he could throw it into reverse and burn rubber speeding off.

She wasn't taking the bait. Instead, she waited behind the car for him to get all the way out.

After a pause, looking discouraged and as if he'd been outmaneuvered, a sturdy-looking, middle-aged man with dark, thinning hair climbed out.

"Afternoon, lady," he said, looking faintly uncomfortable. "You got a problem? Anything you need help with?"

Stella clenched her jaw. She was done with playing games.

"Why are you following me?" she snapped.

He blinked a few times. She could see he was thinking hard and was not yet ready to capitulate.

"Me? Following you?"

"Yes."

"Sorry, lady, you must have the wrong guy. I'm not following anyone. I'm here waiting for a doctor's appointment."

Stella folded her arms.

"You have been following me. I saw your car yesterday and today. In fact, my investigation partner and I both noted it," she bluffed. "We saw the dent on the hood and also the details of your plates. We haven't run them yet, but we will. Being FBI, we're trained to notice tails. Being officers of the law, we don't appreciate interference in our work. My partner's in the police station across the road right now. He's busy charging a suspect. I'm going to call him and tell him to come here as soon as he's done and arrest you so we can charge you for stalking."

Looking purposeful, Stella took out her phone and pretended to dial.

The bluff worked.

"No, no, don't do that, lady. There's no reason to do that," he gabbled.

"There's every reason," Stella said. "We are in the middle of a very serious murder investigation and as such, we need to know why someone might be following us. Hello, Maxwell, I need your help here urgently," she said into the phone.

"Please, don't arrest me," the man said in a low voice, speaking rapidly. He now looked panicked.

Stella looked down at the phone thoughtfully for a while. She could almost sense the man's blood pressure spiking. Finally, she spoke again.

"I'll call you back in a moment," she said, and stabbed at the screen, disconnecting her fake call.

"Okay." She turned to him. "Who are you and why are you following me? And I want the truth. I'm all out of patience with lies today."

"I'm a private investigator," he said.

"Your name?"

"Greg Gibson, of GG Enterprises."

"I assume you know who I am. So why are you stalking me, Greg?"

"It's not stalking, honestly," he appealed. "The truth is that I was asked to observe you by a client."

"Name of?" she asked.

"I also have confidentiality issues on my side," he mumbled.

"Okay, you've had enough chances. I'm bringing you in," Stella snapped. She turned back to her phone and pretended to dial again.

"All right. The client is a Mr. Gordon Marshall," Greg confessed.

"What?" Stella could hear the incredulity in her own voice. The newspaper headline she'd glimpsed yesterday loomed in her mind again.

Her ex-fiancé's family, currently defending themselves against charges of corruption and trafficking. Blaming Stella for their predicament. And now, hiring someone to follow her.

"What did he tell you to do?" she asked.

"If this gets back to Gordon, he'll destroy me," the man said, and she picked up the fear in his voice.

The investigator's admission of how easily Gordon Marshall could annihilate people's lives and careers scared Stella, too. It took an effort for her to reply confidently.

"It won't get back to him from me. I haven't spoken to him since I left their property, back in May."

Greg nodded. "Yes. That's what Mr. Marshall said. That you'd lived with the family for a while and that you had devised false facts about them that you were trying to use against them."

"That's a lie, but go on," Stella invited, feeling angrier by the minute but also fearful of the alternative truth that Gordon was creating.

"Mr. Marshall said that he was trying to save his family from harm."

"Harm? And what exactly did he say I was planning to do?"

She couldn't believe the extent of the lies this man had been fed.

"Well, he didn't say exactly. He just implied that you'd been spreading damaging information."

"That's not the case. And how would following me help to fix that anyway?"

"He wanted me to get some evidence of you doing something irregular," Greg said, now looking embarrassed. "He said that he needed it in order to fight back. He said anything would do. That if I could photograph you doing something wrong in your job it would be best. Any infringement of the law would also work. But I – I mean, I've been watching you quite a bit and I've seen nothing. So far. You've done nothing yet."

Stella stared at him in shock.

This was nothing to do with stopping her from making trouble. The trouble that Gordon had brought upon himself and that she'd uncovered was already there. It wasn't going to go away.

What Gordon Marshall was trying to do was to destroy her in turn. This was a pure revenge move. He was looking for any ammunition to use. And clearly, he was prepared to pay whatever it took in order to do it.

She'd done her best so far in her job, but nobody was perfect. Just yesterday, she'd slandered a fellow officer of the law and let the wrong person know about it. In hostile hands, that information could be dynamite.

Trying to hide how shaken she felt by this, she replied to Greg sharply.

"If I see you again, I'm going to arrest you immediately. As of now, you drop this assignment. Full stop. Or I will find out if you're still on it and I will take action. I'm going to remind you about something you should already know, but perhaps it's slipped your mind. If you want a good career as an investigator, do not mess with the FBI. It will cause trouble on a scale you've never imagined. And you never know when you're going to need us on your side."

Stella had no idea how effectively she could back up the bold threats she was making. But her intimidation tactic had worked because Greg was looking horrified.

"I see, Ms. Fall," he said, finally addressing her by the name he'd obviously been given by Gordon. "I understand. I won't continue and will report back that I've found nothing. I don't want to be in trouble with any law enforcement and I don't want to get on the FBI's wrong side. It was a bad decision to take on this assignment."

Stella was sure that Greg had been persuaded by the money offered.

What could she do? How could she fight this? She had a terrible fear that this was like the many-headed hydra, and that putting a stop to this man was only the first in a series of similar battles.

With nothing more to say to Greg, Stella turned and walked away. As she crossed the road, she tried to convince herself that this didn't matter, and that Gordon was wasting his resources and would never succeed.

But as Stella walked into the busy environment of the New Haven police precinct, it occurred to her that even though she was a law-abiding person, Gordon Marshall was not playing by the same rules. He never had. That was why he was facing these consequences now. Desperate and vindictive, who knew how far he would go in his quest for retribution?

Seeing her arrive, Maxwell raised his head and stared at her, looking worried.

"Roth called," he said. "Something's not going right. He said there was a big problem we needed to discuss, and he sounded really pissed."

"Why?" Stella asked, anxiety surging.

Maxwell shrugged. "He had to go into a meeting and said he'd be unavailable for a couple of hours and would call back as soon as he could. All I know is that we're in deep trouble, and we'd better try and make progress on this case in the meantime."

CHAPTER TWENTY TWO

Stella knew why she and Maxwell were in trouble. Her mind leaped back to that conversation with Carrie. Triggered and emotional, she'd spilled out far too much. She'd given Carrie the ammunition she needed to bring her down.

"It's my fault," she admitted.

"Why?" Maxwell stared at her in surprise.

"I vented about Grover when I called New Haven earlier. I said too much to the wrong person."

"Who's the wrong person?" Maxwell asked.

Stella felt reluctant to name a fellow agent, but Maxwell had to know.

"Carrie Potts."

Maxwell shook his head, confused.

"Why would Potts have issues with any of that? She's FBI, isn't she? A new agent, same as you?"

Stella shook her head. "I don't want to go into details. We were at Quantico together. There's history between us. Potts is from this area. She has connections here. Her mother taught Desiree. And she needled me into saying that I thought Grover was corrupt." Shame filled Stella as she remembered her reckless words.

She suspected that Grover's unhelpful attitude was encouraged, and perhaps even bankrolled, by anxious parents who wanted their sons' reputations to remain undamaged and were prepared to offer incentives to the local police to make sure.

But she shouldn't have said so.

Maxwell made a face. "I think he's corrupt, too, but yes, it probably wasn't the wisest thing to share. Not without proof."

Stella shook her head.

"It was the stupidest thing I could have done. She holds all the power now. She can use it against me. She might already have done that, and Roth now knows. Maxwell, I could be kicked out as a result of this, or at any rate, transferred. I might be facing a lawsuit," Stella explained miserably, noting that Maxwell now looked thoroughly alarmed.

"That can't happen!"

Stella shrugged. "I'll fight it as hard as I can. I'm just saying that I made a mistake and I need to bear the consequences."

She'd have to wait for the explosion. Although she couldn't prevent it, she could make sure Maxwell wouldn't be collateral damage.

"I wish I could have done things differently," she continued. "It's unfair if you end up being affected by this so I'm not going to let that happen."

Maxwell shook his head firmly. "We're partners on the case, Fall. We take the ups and downs together. And now, we need to stop worrying and get back to trying to solve the damned thing. If we can do that, Roth will have more ammo to use in the politics."

Stella felt comforted by his support. He was on her side and right now, that meant everything.

"When I was outside, I spoke to my mentor and asked him for advice," she told Maxwell.

"What did he say?"

Stella pulled out a chair and sat down opposite him.

"He helped me think in a different direction, which was that we should look at who wasn't on the guest list, rather than who was."

Maxwell took a moment to absorb this idea, before nodding thoughtfully.

"That makes sense. If it was preplanned, the killer wouldn't want to be seen, but to sneak in and out. It does open up the field more widely. We might be talking friends of friends, and that list of guests is already long."

"Let's take another look at it," Stella said.

"Here. I printed it out."

Leaning over the desk, Stella looked at the list of names. Maxwell had jotted notes in his neat hand next to some of the entries.

"So who's not on the list? Who wasn't at the party?"

"Mark Halford, Jessica's love interest who slept with Desiree. But he was away," Maxwell replied. "I called his parents earlier, and they confirmed he was at a family function in East Hampton."

"He's cleared, then. Who else?" Stella thought out loud.

"Desiree's husband wasn't at the party," Maxwell said.

"Walter was definitely not the killer. When I interviewed him just now, he said he hasn't had anything to do with the Woods family for nearly two years."

As Stella said the words, she realized there was a discrepancy she'd missed, and hadn't questioned. She saw Maxwell reach the same conclusion.

"Why two years?" Stella asked, now puzzled by the long gap.

"Walter and Desiree divorced about three months ago. That was when he moved to Saratoga Springs. I assumed the split-up was why they no longer socialized with the Woods. That's what they implied," Maxwell frowned.

"They did imply that. But Walter said nearly two years," Stella confirmed, now feeling confused. "We should ask about that. Perhaps there was a reason for it."

"Perhaps they just stopped being friends," Maxwell countered.

"'The timeframe is making me curious. I'm wondering if something happened."

In the back of her mind, a suspicion had started to form. Nearly two years ago – give or take a few months – was when they had the first proof of Desiree's affairs. Had this been a contributing factor, Stella wondered. She was starting to see a picture.

Stella dialed Walter's number. After a few rings, Walter answered, and she put the call onto speaker so that Maxwell could also hear.

"Walter Jardine."

He sounded breathless, as if he'd grabbed the phone and rushed out of a meeting room when he saw Stella on the line.

"Sorry to interrupt you again. I want to confirm a detail."

"Sure. Go ahead," Walter said.

"When was the last time you and Desiree saw the Woods family socially?"

Walter paused. "Nearly two years ago. I think I told you that already. We were invited to Carolyn's birthday party, but not to Duncan's, or to their Christmas party that year. Desiree held a big birthday bash for her fortieth, but they weren't there. I remember noting their absence, but never got around to asking if she'd invited them or not."

"So you don't know why they suddenly lost touch with you?"

Walter sighed. "Yes. I'm afraid I do."

Stella exchanged a glance with Maxwell. So there was a reason – and not one that Walter was happy with?

"Why?" Stella asked.

"It was because of me," Walter admitted.

"How's that?" That wasn't what she'd expected him to say at all.

"Because I was not a fun person," Walter said wryly.

Stella couldn't believe what she was hearing.

"You're saying that the Woods stopped inviting you to their events because you weren't fun?"

Walter sighed. "That's what Desiree said."

"What was the context?" Stella asked.

"When I mentioned to her, this past January, that we hadn't received an invite to Carolyn's party yet, and I wondered if we were going, she lashed out at me."

"Really?" Stella said. She was surprised by that, because it didn't sound characteristic of Desiree.

"Yes. She said it was my fault we hadn't been invited. That I was the reason we were off their guest list and that she was sick of going to events with me and having me leave early – well, early for her being at around midnight as she liked to party well into the small hours. She said I was a party pooper and a boring person, and that if things carried on like this, we'd have no friends."

Stella felt shocked by this. She had not guessed there was a vicious side to her and that she would lash out at her husband in this way.

"What was your response?"

"I didn't really respond," Walter said, sounding miserable. "It seemed unreasonable to me, but I didn't think it was worth getting into a fight over. She was upset, so I thought it was best to leave her. But it was hurtful. I didn't expect to be attacked like that. It was one of the first signs I had that there was a real rift between us."

"I'm sorry to hear that. Thank you for the information," Stella said.

She put the phone down feeling dumbstruck.

It seemed that every time she spoke to Walter, he ended up giving her more unexpected facts in that calm, measured voice. This was highly significant.

Walter had asked. Desiree had attacked.

Walter had backed down, hurt and confused.

"That sounds irrational. There must have been other reasons," Maxwell said.

Stella was sure that the excuse Desiree had provided was not the real reason. They would have to go digging for the real reason, and the only people who would know were Mr. and Mrs. Woods.

"We need to ask the Woods about it. And while we're on the subject, let's check where they were on that night," she said.

She remembered Clem's words about who had not been at the party. Carolyn and Duncan Woods had not been at their son's party. They'd stated that they'd been away. But now, Stella realized she didn't even know where they had been.

Maxwell grimaced. "We slipped up there. We should have confirmed that much sooner. Let's go back to Putnam now and re-look at that evidence. They did mention a venue in one of their statements, I remember."

They stood up, collected their things, and rushed for the car.

As Maxwell drove, Stella started to feel more and more suspicious as she thought about Desiree's outburst.

In all the interviews and all the character reports that she'd obtained so far, Desiree had not struck her as a vicious person. She'd been misguided sometimes. Increasingly reckless for sure. Irresponsible, and becoming more so. But Stella had not heard any other witness describe a vicious or nasty streak and she didn't think it was characteristic of Desiree at all.

She was eager to find out what had caused this defensive backlash. Guilt was the emotion that first came to mind.

Why had Desiree been so badly triggered by a guilty reaction to this innocent question of why they had stopped seeing the Woods, and could this hold the key to her murder?

Stella felt certain it did.

CHAPTER TWENTY THREE

With Maxwell driving like a demon, he and Stella arrived at the Putnam precinct in less than twenty minutes. They rushed into the precinct, where they were met by the surprised stare of the same desk sergeant who'd admitted them earlier that day.

"Afternoon. We're back," Stella said briskly.

The sergeant looked perturbed.

"Again?" he asked.

"Yes. We need to view the case file a second time."

The sergeant hesitated.

"Detective Grover is out. He stated very clearly that nobody was to access the back offices without him being present."

Stella wasn't going to play this game.

"If Grover doesn't want us to use the back offices, then you can bring the case file to us. It's the Desiree Jardine murder file. We need to review one document. You can oversee us while we read it. I don't mind that at all." Then she added as threateningly as she could, "If you don't allow us to access information on a case that we are officially involved in, I can guarantee there will be consequences. For you. Do you want to be up on charges of obstruction of justice, because this is what it amounts to?"

The sergeant looked startled, and then very worried, as if he now had two choices and both of them would end up with him in trouble. Stella thought he was afraid of Grover. However, at this moment, the trouble from the FBI was more real and immediate.

"You can go through. Just please, be quick," he said.

He got up and unlocked the interleading door.

Stella rushed through with Maxwell close behind.

The office was empty. The team must be out, either on routine duty or else following up on the carjacking case that had pulled all the personnel away from the murder investigation.

That was fine by her. The case file still lay on the table where they'd left it. Nobody had bothered to put it away, although she noticed that the filing cabinets at the back of the room, which had been half-open last time they were there, were now locked up.

"Right," Maxwell said. "Let's see the details in this statement."

Stella felt as if she was finally gaining traction in this case. They'd uncovered an inconsistency, both in the timeframe of when the Woods and Jardines had stopped seeing each other, and then in Desiree's reaction when questioned why.

She couldn't wait to dig deeper and find out what was behind this. She paged through the file until she reached the brief statements from Duncan and Carolyn Woods.

"We were on a weekend getaway but left at about eight-thirty a.m. on Sunday after being unable to get hold of Clint," Duncan's statement read. Brief in the extreme, Stella thought. Any competent investigating officer would have pushed for more information. Unless that officer was trying to protect the parents and shield their fine young son who'd thrown the party.

Luckily, there were a few more details in Carolyn's statement.

"We had a two-night stay planned at Riverside Retreat. We left for the stay on Saturday morning. We planned to return on Monday morning, but when we were unable to contact our son on Sunday morning, we decided to drive back, in case something had gone wrong."

Quickly, Stella photographed the entire statement on her phone, just in case there was any other useful information in the brief outline.

"Riverside Retreat?" Maxwell said with a question in his voice.

"A retreat? Sounds like a spiritual destination," Stella said. She agreed that the name was intriguing. The Woods hadn't struck her as spiritual people, particularly Duncan. All the more reason to confirm what it was.

"Let's look it up online. Then we can see where it is and check the travel timelines," Maxwell said.

Stella scooted around to his side of the desk and joined him there, staring intently at his laptop as he searched the name of the venue. Their knees were touching, but she barely noticed. All her attention was focused on exploring this new avenue.

"Here you go," Maxwell said. "Riverside Retreat. It's in Brookfield, Massachusetts. That would be about an hour's drive from the Woods' home, which would fit in with their timeline of getting back."

"Let's see the website?" Stella said, curious to know if her guess about a spiritual retreat was correct.

"Here it is."

Maxwell clicked on the name.

The screen illuminated into a pastel symphony of peace and beauty. Weeping willows, flowing water, and a stately Georgian building, set among wooded surroundings.

"What is it?"

Maxwell shook his head. "They don't give much info." He moved the mouse around impatiently.

Stella felt more and more confused as she waited for the usual 'About Us, Bookings, Rates,' menu. But nothing came up. All she could see was a small text box saying, 'Inquire Now,' with a contact number and a physical address.

"How do we know they were even at this place? And what is it? Surely a spiritual retreat would market themselves as such?" Maxwell asked.

"Maybe it's a rehab center," Stella guessed again. "A highly discreet one? Perhaps they were visiting someone there?"

Maxwell shook his head. "Spiritual retreat, rehab center. Either way, it seems out of the ordinary, and we need to check it out. Find out if they were really there, and if so, what they were doing."

"Try calling?" Stella said.

Maxwell dialed the number.

"Hello." He waited. "Yes. I'm Agent Maxwell from the FBI. I'd like to find out about your place and confirm the arrival and departure time of a certain guest."

He waited some more, tapping his fingers on the desk.

Then, with a sigh, he disconnected.

"Receptionist says she can't give out any information without her manager's say-so. And surprise, surprise, the manager is not in the office right now. We're going to get nowhere this way."

He glanced at his watch and his mouth tightened. Stella knew what he was thinking. She felt the same, with a sense of panic, as she glanced at her own watch. It was already quarter to four in the afternoon.

An hour's drive there and back felt like a long time to spend in the car, but they needed to check out this place in person. This was an important alibi to confirm, and so far, they'd taken the Woods' word for where they'd been. Stella imagined how Roth would focus on that omission.

At that moment, the interleading door banged open and Detective Grover marched in.

He looked on the warpath. Bad temper crackled from him.

"What the hell's going on?" he snapped. "Why are you in here again?"

"Good afternoon, Detective," Stella said politely, even though her blood pressure spiked at his rude defensiveness. "We're still working on the case."

"Any personnel available yet to assist us?" Maxwell asked pointedly.

"You will not be getting my assistance!" Grover blustered. "I'm done with your interfering in this matter. You're traumatizing families. You're wasting my staff's time! And I'm aware – fully aware – of what you've been up to. Your unethical behavior will have consequences!"

Fear chilled Stella at those words. Grover hadn't said, but he had strongly hinted, that Carrie Potts was taking this further, and had told him all of her slanderous accusations.

This was going so horribly wrong.

"I'm sorry you feel this way," she said, wondering with a sick feeling whether Carrie had actually recorded her words during their phone conversation. She could have easily done so. That would have the most damaging results. Stella cringed away from the thought of Roth's disappointment and anger.

And worse still, despite making a lasting enemy out of Grover and putting herself in line for a potential lawsuit, they hadn't made real progress on the case.

"We're heading out now to confirm some details," she said politely, trying not to show that she felt literally full of despair, and they were pinning all their hopes on checking out this discrepancy.

Grover's words about the cold case were proving to be so prophetic. So far, anyway.

"Come on. Let's go," Maxwell muttered.

They marched out. Stella felt Grover's angry glare burning a hole in her back. He was furious, and on the warpath for revenge. And they had nothing to bring to the table that would appease Roth.

Time was ticking by. The golden hour that represented the best chance for solving the case was swiftly passing. Stella didn't want to think that this trip to Riverside Retreat might represent their last hope.

But at that moment, it sure felt like it.

CHAPTER TWENTY FOUR

Riverside Retreat looked even grander in real life than it had done on the website picture, Stella thought, as they sped up to the main gate. The building was palatial, and it was set in exquisite, rolling countryside.

"Can't be a rehab center. No fences," Maxwell observed, as they drove up the long, winding driveway and parked in the paved lot, alongside a few luxury vehicles.

Stella nodded. Maxwell's observation was correct. The gates at the bottom of the driveway were wide open and there were no guards or security personnel in attendance. Rehab centers always had walls, or fences, as well as some sort of security in place.

The front door stood wide. From beyond, warm lighting illuminated the reception hall, giving it a welcoming feel.

Stella walked in, wondering what she would find, and whether it would be relevant in any way. If not, they'd wasted two precious hours. Roth would surely be wrapping up his meeting soon and could call at any moment.

Inside, a thick teal carpet led the way to a polished wooden reception counter. A smiling young receptionist greeted them, clearly jumping to the wrong conclusion about Stella and Maxwell.

"Good afternoon! Are you checking in?" She glanced down at her computer, clearly not seeing an open booking for today. "Or are you here for the introductory tour?"

Stella decided to seize the opportunity to learn about this place first-hand.

"We'd love a quick introduction, as you don't seem to have any information on your website," she said, glad that it wasn't a lie and that she could drop the FBI bombshell afterwards without feeling she'd misrepresented herself.

"Of course! And no, we don't market on our website at all, for reasons of discretion. We're purely word of mouth, which is how I guess you might have heard about us?"

Stella said nothing in reply, feeling more and more mystified. Smiling encouragingly, the receptionist walked from behind the desk and headed across the reception hall to the far wall.

As they followed her, Stella glanced at Maxwell who widened his eyes slightly and gave an almost imperceptible shake of his head to show he was as confused as she was.

Displayed on the wall, Stella saw a number of large, framed photos.

"This is our photographic gallery," the receptionist smiled, gesturing to the photo of a palatial bedroom suite with a lounge area and a mini study. "This is a picture of our luxury accommodation. Most of our guests choose separate rooms while they work through their journey. We can offer these adjacent to each other or else in different wings, depending on what you prefer."

"I see," Stella said, and she was starting to, as the receptionist progressed to the second photo of a plate of artfully arranged food.

"Our daily rate includes three gourmet meals which can be enjoyed either in the suite of your choice, or in one of our dining areas. You receive wine with dinner and can purchase any other drinks. Tea, coffee, snacks, and cookies are available at all times in your room. Most of our couples prefer to dine together but if you choose not to, this can also be arranged. Our chef's menu is compiled daily with several delicious alternatives, and is based on local, seasonal produce. Of course, we cater for all dietary preferences."

With a flourish, the receptionist moved onto the third photo of an earnest-faced man sitting opposite a couch, where a man and woman occupied different ends.

"Counseling and therapy are obviously the primary reasons why guests attend Riverside Retreat, and we offer up to three different relationship repair sessions daily, from our resident experts. These include counseling sessions from our two leading psychologists which can be done individually or as a couple, as well as sessions with a sex therapist, an anger management specialist, a life coach, and a spiritual wellness adviser. We have such excellent results from this expert team! We understand that our clients come here in a vulnerable state, with serious and sometimes long-term problems, and our goal is to help you repair, resolve, and rebuild your relationship in a safe, supportive, and luxurious setting."

Moving on to the next picture of an aquamarine infinity pool, she continued. "Outside of the therapy, we offer hiking, swimming, sauna, yoga, spa treatments, and tennis so you can enjoy your stay and relax while you are here."

Stella had heard enough. She'd gotten the gist of this place and needed no further explanation. What she'd found out was surprising and intriguing.

"Thank you so much for the overview. I'd like to speak to your manager urgently. I have some questions," Stella said.

"Let me take you through."

The receptionist led them to the opposite side of the reception hall and tapped discreetly on a white-painted door.

She opened it and ushered them inside.

The older, dark-haired and worldlier-looking woman sitting behind the ornate wooden desk stood up.

"Welcome!" she said with a warm smile as the door closed softly behind them.

Then, looking from Maxwell to Stella and back again, she hesitated. Stella guessed she was picking up what the receptionist hadn't – that they were not typical prospective clients, and that they looked too young, too poor, and probably had a few other visible red flags as well.

"How can I help?" she said, more formally this time.

It was time to reveal who they were.

"We're FBI agents Fall and Maxwell," Stella said. "We came here to confirm what Riverside Retreat is about, and to inquire about guests who stayed here recently."

As Stella spoke, she saw the manager go a few shades paler.

"We have confidentiality issues," she muttered, but Maxwell shook his head.

"We're investigating a murder that was committed at the home of one of your guests, while they were on a stay here. So we need to confirm certain facts."

"All right," the manager capitulated. Watching her, Stella was sure she already knew what had happened. Perhaps she'd heard through the grapevine, or from the Woods family directly. At any rate, she was astute enough to know that she should cooperate now.

"It's Duncan and Carolyn Woods," Stella explained.

"Yes. They arrived Saturday morning. It was supposed to be a weekend stay but they checked out on Sunday."

Stella wanted to get an idea of what the logistics had been.

"Did they choose separate rooms?" she asked.

The manager nodded. "Separate rooms in separate wings."

"When did they book?"

"A couple of weeks ago. It's their second stay here. They spent four days here last November too."

"Thank you," Stella said.

She felt motivated all over again by what they had learned. It was clear that the Woods had been experiencing ongoing problems in their marriage.

And they had booked separate rooms, in separate wings.

That meant, potentially, either of them could have left during the night, driven home, murdered Desiree, and been back in their room by the early morning without anyone being the wiser.

Furthermore, they'd only made the booking two weeks ago, so this had been done after the party had been organized. Had one of them been looking to create an alibi?

"Do you have a night receptionist?" Stella asked. "If someone left this place during the night, would any staff have seen?"

The manager shook her head.

"At night, we have a butler on call, but he's not in full-time attendance at the front desk. The gate at the bottom of the drive is closed after dark, but all guests have a remote to open it. Some guests go out to eat in the nearby town and get back late. Some need to leave at odd hours if there's a problem back home. In that case, they just drop the remote in the post box."

"Do you have cameras on site?" She hadn't seen any on the way in.

"No. We've never had the need for them," the manager said, sounding apologetic. "We found guests are comfortable with total privacy without any surveillance. In any case, we only work through referrals and word of mouth, and we have an excellent security company who patrols the area."

Feeling determined to approach this from every angle, Stella continued.

"Tell me more about the Woods. Why did they book in? What were the problems they needed to address? Was there a particular problem?"

The manager pressed her lips together for a moment.

"I'm sorry, but I cannot give you that information. It's privileged. In any case, people's relationship journeys are not simple. They are complex. There is seldom one issue."

Stella nodded reluctantly.

"On Saturday night, did they act normally? Did you notice anything unusual about their behavior?" she asked.

"Saturday, they dined together in one of our private dining areas, the Fireplace Room. They seemed to enjoy their meal. There were no complaints. After that, I think they both went to their bedrooms. But this is not unusual. Our guests will sometimes have a drink at the bar after dinner, but in this countryside setting, and with such busy days, most people do turn in early and get up early."

Stella couldn't think of anything else they needed to ask, but she had learned enough. Now, they needed to get back to Putnam, as fast as they could. It was suspicious that the Woods hadn't mentioned their marriage was going through difficulties or explained where they had been. Given Desiree's previous behavior and the fact she'd been murdered, this was now very relevant.

As they drove out of Riverside Retreat, Maxwell's phone rang. Stella saw with her heart plummeting that it was Roth.

Maxwell pressed the button, looking resigned.

Roth's voice filled the car and Stella could hear immediately that he was both angry and annoyed.

"Maxwell. Two things. Firstly, did you or Fall speak to the press regarding this case?"

The press? Stella glanced at Maxwell, feeling surprised by the question. Why was Roth asking this?

"I haven't spoken to the press at all," Maxwell said.

"Nor me," Stella added.

Roth sighed, frustrated.

"There's an article published in Putnam News Online today. It mentions the murder and quotes Detective Grover as saying – I'll read from the web article, *"We have been experiencing a surge in random crime in this area. Within two days, a murder and a carjacking have left one resident dead, and another seriously injured. We are following up on all available leads, but appeal to all residents to tighten up on their home security. If house parties are held, the home should not be left open at night, as it can attract opportunistic criminal elements. Attention should also be paid to the guest list, and people should ensure no uninvited guests gain access to the premises. The Putnam Police Department is just a phone call away at any time to assist with managing these situations."*

"That's it?" Maxwell said.

Stella felt shocked. Grover was misleading the media completely. His stance was very clearly all about protecting the locals and deflecting the blame elsewhere.

“That’s it,” Roth agreed. “The article implies the killer was a random, transient criminal. No mention of the FBI being involved. The university has already been calling me in a panic, asking me if we’re still handling the case.”

“We weren’t contacted by the journalist,” Maxwell said. “I doubt Grover even gave them our number. He doesn’t want us involved.”

Stella could imagine Roth shaking his head in frustration.

“We’re definitely on the wrong foot with Grover. Because there’s another issue now that you two have caused. He called me and told me about it, furiously angry. When he explained it, I was also furious. You acted irresponsibly, and I want answers from you. You in particular, Fall.”

“Answers on what?” Maxwell asked, sounding tense.

Stella felt her stomach twist as she waited for Roth’s response and for the hammer blow to fall.

“I’m about to walk into a press conference, so I can’t discuss this now. In any case, it’s serious enough that we need to meet in person. For now – Fall, Maxwell, just focus on the job. Solve this case. I don’t want any side issues taking precedence and delaying things.”

Sounding at the end of his tether, Roth abruptly disconnected.

Stella took a deep breath.

She never imagined she’d land in such trouble. She wasn’t sure how much Roth had heard, or what version he’d been told. But one thing was for sure, Maxwell was not at fault.

“Maxwell, I need to take the blame for this. Not you. You did nothing wrong. I need to fight this on my own,” she insisted.

Maxwell shook his head. “I can’t believe Roth’s not taking our side on this. Agents need to stick together. And that’s what I’m going to do,” he said firmly.

Stella appreciated his stance, but she knew it wouldn’t hold water with Roth. When it was time for the meeting she was now dreading, she would have to face the disaster she’d created, and its consequences, alone.

CHAPTER TWENTY FIVE

At six-thirty p.m., Stella and Maxwell arrived at the townhouse where the Woods were still residing. She climbed out of the car, feeling a mixture of relief and dread that Roth still hadn't called back. She guessed the press conference was lengthy, and there might be numerous interviews.

This meant a stay of execution for her. She'd still be facing major trouble but at least in the meantime, they might make progress with the case. Hopefully that would mean Maxwell wouldn't share the blame.

With any luck, this interview would change the course of their investigation. Let something go right at last, she pleaded to herself, as she climbed out of the car and walked with Maxwell to the front door.

They hadn't called the Woods to say they were coming back. Both of them had agreed the element of surprise would be critical.

When Duncan Woods opened the door, he did indeed look surprised. He was wearing a pair of jogging shorts, as if he'd just come back from a run, and a gray sweater which Stella guessed he'd pulled on over his running shirt.

"What are you doing here?" he said. There was a note of defensiveness in his voice that hadn't been there before. Last time, he'd accepted their presence as he'd been seething with righteous anger over his son's irresponsible actions. This time, he seemed resentful.

"We have a few more questions," Maxwell said.

Duncan hesitated. He clearly didn't want the agents to come in, but equally obviously couldn't think of a valid reason why not.

"Sure," he said grudgingly after having abandoned the internal battle. "Come this way."

The blare of the television was audible as he led the way into the luxurious, large lounge Stella remembered from before. Both Clint and his mother were watching a talent show, sitting side by side on the leather settee. The singer's high, melodious voice and the roars of applause must have drowned out the sounds of their arrival.

They looked up, and Stella saw identical expressions of shock written on their faces.

Clint reached out and snapped the TV off. An expectant and uncomfortable silence descended.

Stella walked over to a chair and sat down. A moment later, Maxwell did the same. Duncan Woods remained standing near the door.

"What is this?" Carolyn asked, sounding hesitant and scared. "Why are you back? This is our family time. Last time, you called first."

Clint didn't look at them. He stared downward, his gaze fixed on the TV remote as if it represented a portal to a better world.

"We have more questions to ask. Since this is a very urgent murder investigation, we don't always have time to call ahead," Maxwell explained in the same brisk tone he'd used earlier. "I'm sure we will have your cooperation, of course?"

"Of course," Carolyn Woods said quietly.

"Well, can you hurry?" Duncan said in a louder and more aggressive tone.

"Mr. Woods, we'd like to question you first," Stella said.

"Go on," Duncan placed his hands on his hips. It was a threatening, dominant gesture. He still hadn't sat down.

"Where can we speak in private?" Stella asked.

That question seemed to trigger Duncan.

"Private? I'm not rearranging our whole evening just because you now want to divide us, and most likely try and get different versions out of us. We've heard exactly how your strategy works and I'm not falling for it. Anything you have to say to me, you can say in front of my family. They can hear your questions and my replies," he thundered.

Stella heard Detective Grover behind every angry word. She had absolutely no doubt that the Woods family had been well briefed by the protective police officer who was proving to be their nemesis.

"Would you like to sit?" she invited the angry father.

"No. I'll stand," he snapped.

"All right," Stella said, wondering how Duncan would react when he found out the direction this questioning was going to take. He seemed far more volatile than she'd expected. He looked as if he'd be triggered by the smallest thing, and what they were about to discuss was certainly not a small thing.

"We found out that you and your wife have been working on your marriage. As in, seeking therapy for it. And that's where you were, this past weekend. At Riverside Retreat, which specializes in the healing of problems between couples."

Stella was right. Duncan's face had turned to thunder. He glared at them in silence.

Now Clint was looking from one parent to the other, unsure and surprised by this. Stella wondered if he'd known about the problems, or about the therapy. How much of what was about to be unleashed would be a shock to Clint?

Carolyn was the one who finally answered, smiling nervously.

"Yes, we love to go there. We find it refreshes our relationship," she said.

"We already confirmed with the venue," Stella said, not in the mood for half-truths. "They said you booked separate rooms in separate wings."

Carolyn tried another wobbly smile.

"It's not like it sounds. You see, I have great difficulty sleeping when I'm away from home, so it's what we usually do, so that Duncan gets undisturbed rest. I mean, I – we wouldn't have minded adjacent rooms at all. They just happened to place us in separate wings."

Stella was taking note of the fact that Carolyn had answered all the questions so far. Not one question had been answered by Duncan Woods. He was glowering at them with his lips pressed together.

Stella felt his reaction was significant.

"Mrs. Woods, I appreciate your input. But from this point, the questions I am asking are directed at your husband," she said firmly.

Carolyn nodded apologetically as Stella turned to Duncan and continued.

"You stopped talking to the Jardines nearly two years ago and cut them off from your social circle. We thought initially it was because they got divorced. But that happened more recently," Stella said. "So there must have been another reason why, suddenly, after Carolyn's birthday party nearly two years ago, the Jardines were never invited to another of your events again."

"I guess we just drifted apart, Carolyn said hastily.

"Ma'am, your turn for questioning will come," Stella reminded her.

"Sorry," she said in a breathy voice.

Duncan had still not spoken. But now, Stella noticed, the righteous anger in his demeanor had ebbed. He was looking haunted. He was looking as if this was a catastrophe in the making.

“My guess is different.” Stella said to him in a firm voice. “My guess is that you had an affair with Desiree, and your wife found out, and that blew the friendship between your families right out of the water.”

“And caused lasting problems in your marriage,” Maxwell added harshly.

Behind her, Stella heard Clint’s shocked gasp.

“I did no such thing!” Duncan shouted. He was showing classic signs of stress. His face was tense, and he was shifting from foot to foot as if he’d like nothing more than to march out of the room.

Remembering the stress signals Carolyn had shown last time, Stella glanced at her. Sure enough, she was twining her fingers together, fidgeting nervously just as she’d done the previous time when she felt under pressure.

“I believe you did. And it will be in your interests to disclose it now,” Stella threatened him.

“Why would I sleep with her? She was a family friend, nothing more! I’m a married man!”

Stella pressed on, needing to crack through his shell of denial.

“Because she was needy. She was unfulfilled. She was a very attractive, dynamic person. There was most definitely something untamed and rebellious about her that appealed to men. She cared nothing for society’s conventions. And maybe she caught you in a moment where you felt that was what you needed,” Stella suggested.

There was a resounding silence in the lounge.

Yet again, Carolyn Woods broke it, clearing her throat loudly.

“Yes,” she said in a voice quivering with stress. “It’s true. He did do that.”

Stella sat bolt upright, exchanging a glance with Maxwell.

Finally, they had a confession that pointed to a powerful motive for murder.

Duncan turned to his wife, looking so furious that Maxwell jumped to his feet. Stella saw him grab the handcuffs on his belt and knew he was ready to restrain the wrathful husband if this was needed.

Duncan began shouting, in harsh, unsteady tones. “What? How can you say that? Are you crazy, Carolyn?”

Clint leaned forward, tugging at his father’s arm.

“Dad, Dad, calm down,” he pleaded. He looked appalled, although Stella wasn’t sure whether it was due to the bombshell of the confession, or to his father’s blatant display of fury. On seeing his son’s face, Duncan made a supreme effort to control his rage. He lapsed into silence, breathing hard.

Then, in a small, scared voice, Carolyn continued.

"You probably suspect one of us as being her killer because that happened. But your theory is not correct. There is far more to this background than you know about. You need to hear the full story. It will help you to understand."

"And what is the full story?" Stella asked, turning to her.

"Perhaps Clint can leave the room?" Carolyn suggested, turning to her son. "This is not for his ears."

Clint looked startled. He got up and walked out of the side door, glancing back as if he was reluctant to go. Only when he'd closed the door did Carolyn continue.

"It started with me. I was the first one to have an affair. I was the one whose actions damaged our marriage," she said in a small, shaky voice.

Duncan drew in a sharp breath at these words, but Stella's attention was focused on Carolyn.

"I slept with a physiotherapist who was treating me for a hamstring injury," she explained. "It didn't last long, as he moved out of state a few months later. Then Duncan had a brief affair with Desiree, while I was seeing another lover on and off for a month or two. He was someone who worked with a charity where I was helping out. Duncan and I were at a stage where we had drifted apart and, eventually, we reached the point where we had to make a choice."

She wasn't looking at Stella while she spoke. She was looking down at her hands, her face reddening, as if telling this story was difficult for her. Behind her, Stella could hear Duncan's harsh breathing.

Stella felt puzzled by this story. She'd never guessed that there was so much complex background to this relationship. She hadn't thought of Carolyn as a cheater, but she had clearly been wrong. This relationship hadn't had just one fault line. Carolyn was telling her there had been multiple cracks in its façade.

"What choice were you making?" Maxwell asked.

"Were we going to split up, or were we going to try again and make it work?" Carolyn said. "Eventually, Duncan admitted to his affair, and I felt so relieved. It was as if he'd given me permission to admit to mine. We put everything on the table. I can't say that the information was a surprise to either of us, because we were so distanced in our marriage. But we decided that we would make it work. We talked about it together. We sought therapy and attended weekly sessions. We booked regular getaways at places like Riverside Retreat. And we decided to stop seeing the Jardines," Carolyn spilled out her story, just about sobbing with stress.

"Why did you do that?" Stella asked.

Carolyn paused, cleared her throat again, and then managed to gather herself before continuing. Her face was deeply flushed.

"Simply because we would both have felt self-conscious about socializing with Walter, after what had happened, since he didn't know about it and all the rest of us now did. Neither Duncan nor I have fought recently. We reconciled. And I never bore Desiree a grudge at all. I see her periodically. We go to the same hairdresser and beauty salon. We always greet each other if we see each other there, and there's no bad blood."

"Okay," Stella.

"In fact, I was thankful to her because she was the catalyst that helped us both change," Carolyn continued. "And we've been working on our marriage since then. Forgiveness has been an important part of our journey. Forgiving ourselves. Forgiving the mistakes. Forgiving each other. We're healing. Together. And we're not responsible for this murder. Please believe us."

Now, finally, she raised her head and stared at Stella in appeal.

Stella wasn't buying this theory. She didn't trust that the Woods were healing. And she didn't understand Carolyn's extreme nervousness. Something wasn't adding up.

She was not going to leave until she'd dug deeper into the strange dynamics that were playing out between this couple.

CHAPTER TWENTY SIX

"Is that all, agents?" Duncan Woods asked, staring hard at Stella. "I trust you're satisfied now? Can you leave us to get on with our evening in peace?"

"Alright." Deciding to see what happened if she bluffed, Stella shifted her feet underneath her to stand up.

As she did that, she noticed a subtle change in both the Woods' expressions.

Carolyn closed her eyes briefly and it was only when her face relaxed, that Stella realized the excessive amount of tension she'd been holding. Duncan, on the other hand, looked frantic with impatience, as if he held an invisible timer that was counting down the seconds to their departure.

These reactions were not normal. They were too eager to see her and Maxwell go. This definitely meant there was something they were still hiding.

Divide and conquer might be the best way to explore this further, Stella thought.

Smoothly, she continued. "We won't be much longer at all and will leave as soon as we have tested this version. Mr. Woods, I must now ask you to move elsewhere in the house, so that we can question you on your own."

Maxwell shot her a startled glance, but it was nothing compared to the change in Duncan Woods' demeanor.

He drew himself up, enraged. His hands bunched together. His face flushed deeply, and his mouth contorted.

"This is all your fault!" he yelled.

But not at Stella. His words, and his anger, were directed at his wife.

"How can you say such things, Carolyn?" Duncan raged, his emotions now laid bare. "How can you tell them all this? Are you some kind of idiot? You should have just shut the hell up!"

Stella stared at him in shock. This reaction was completely unexpected. Duncan's shouted insults had just shattered the amicable resolution scenario.

There was more to this after all. This marriage wasn't all unicorns and rainbows and happy endings, as Carolyn had so earnestly implied.

"I'm saying this because I must," Carolyn insisted, her voice shaking but her tone intense. "This is a murder investigation, Duncan. This is the FBI asking questions. It's our life. Our son's future. Don't be a fool. We have to explain."

"You are only going to get us into deeper trouble," Duncan thundered, causing Stella's gaze to swivel between them, taking in the visible conflict that now flared between husband and wife. She wasn't sure why Duncan's behavior was escalating this way. He seemed to have been completely triggered by his wife's version. Furthermore, he was providing a real-time contradiction of Carolyn's statement that no fighting had recently occurred in the marriage. She was watching one, right now.

"That's enough," Maxwell said, clearly losing patience with this husband-wife friction. "Mr. Woods, we're going to bring you into the police station and question you there."

"What?" Duncan yelled. "You can't do that! You have no reason to think I committed this crime!"

"Your aggressive behavior is escalating to a point where we can't get any clear answers from you in this environment," Maxwell countered reasonably. "We have ample reasons to question you. You have a clear motive to have committed this crime, and you had the opportunity to do it as you were alone on that night."

"I refuse! This is totally unnecessary," Duncan blustered, but now Stella heard doubt and fear in his tone.

"Mr. Woods, you can come with us willingly, or you can come in handcuffs. But we need you to get into the car now," Maxwell insisted.

"Screw that!" Duncan had clearly reached breaking point.

"Mr. Woods, please comply," sick of his ranting, Stella stood up and faced him. She saw the fear, ugly in his eyes. It lurked behind his aggression, fueling it. Why was he so afraid, she wondered, as she walked toward the door. That was what they needed to pinpoint.

"Don't you tell me what to do," Duncan threatened. As Stella passed, he lunged toward her and shoved her hard.

Taken by surprise, she stumbled to the side, twisting to face him in case she needed to defend against an attack. She didn't know if he would have tried, because Maxwell was too fast for him.

"That's enough!" Maxwell grabbed Duncan by his arm and pulled him away from Stella, looking furious at the tall man's disrespectful abuse. Teetering on a knife-edge of self-control, Duncan lost it. He raised his other arm, fist bunched.

"You guys are interfering in our lives! You're looking for scapegoats. This crime will never be solved. Get the hell out of my home!"

Leaping forward, Stella grabbed his wrist just as he tried to take a swing at Maxwell. She was amazed by how strong Duncan was. He swore and shouted, trying to rip his wrist away as he struggled.

Had he used this strength against Desiree in the same blind fury, she wondered.

Stella was not letting go. She hung onto him for all that she was worth. Duncan might be taller and more powerful than her, but he was not strong enough to wrench himself free from her determined grasp. Especially now that Maxwell had the cuffs over his other wrist.

Duncan kicked out, furious and panicked, aiming his swinging foot once again at Stella. She jackknifed out of the way of his hard leather shoe and Maxwell shoved Duncan up against the wall chest-first. He slammed into it, shouting in pain and shock as Maxwell yanked his other hand behind him.

"Stop this now! I demand to call my lawyer. This is abuse!" Duncan yelled.

Carolyn's high-pitched cries of fear formed a wavering descant to her husband's roars.

"Please don't hurt him! Just let him go! Please don't arrest him! Agents, I swear our family is innocent of this," she begged. "Duncan, just calm down! Calm down and think about what I said, please."

"Ma'am, you must also calm down. We're not arresting him. We are taking him in for questioning. He won't cooperate, so we are using force," Stella explained breathlessly, trying her best to stop the situation from exploding totally.

The side door banged open, and Clint peered round, looking horrified.

"Dad!" Clint called. "Dad, just go with them. Don't fight them, Dad, it's a federal offense to do that, we learned it in school!"

Now that Duncan was firmly handcuffed, or perhaps because his son's words had sunk in, he had stopped struggling. His fit of rage was under control again, but it had been very educational for Stella to watch it. She now knew that Duncan Woods lost control easily, and that he defaulted to physical violence when under stress.

Those were important facts.

"Now come!" Maxwell grabbed the cuffs, turned Duncan roughly toward the doorway, and shepherded him out.

"Call our lawyer!" Duncan shouted to his wife. "Brief him on what's happened. I'm not spending a night in jail for no reason!"

"I'll call him straight away," Carolyn replied.

Outside, the night was cold and breezy. Stella opened the car door and Maxwell shoved Duncan inside, down on the seat. After his earlier behavior, Stella knew those cuffs weren't coming off, and that he had an uncomfortable ride ahead.

Before she climbed inside, she stood for a moment, breathing in the cool, fresh air. It felt refreshing after the oppressive atmosphere in that beautifully decorated townhouse. There had been tensions on all sides in there, and she still didn't understand their full complexity.

Hopefully, with Duncan Woods now away from his wife and son and in their custody, they would be able to learn the truth of what had really happened on that night.

CHAPTER TWENTY SEVEN

When Stella and Maxwell arrived at the Putnam police station, Stella saw to her dismay that Detective Grover was standing outside the front entrance, as if guarding it. His arms were folded, and he looked absolutely furious at seeing Duncan Woods emerge from the car.

Stella felt certain that Carolyn Woods had called him to explain what was happening.

"What is this?" Grover snapped.

"We're bringing a suspect in for questioning," Maxwell told him shortly. He kept a tight grip on the cuffs as he hustled Duncan inside.

"He's a suspect?" Grover asked incredulously. "Our team cleared him immediately. What are the grounds for your suspicion? And why is he handcuffed?"

"There are no grounds," Duncan said in a rapid, tense voice. "I can't believe this is happening. It's a total abuse of power."

"You assaulted an officer of the law," Maxwell said angrily.

"I pushed her!" Duncan protested. "That was all I did until you started attacking me."

"We need an interview room. Which one can we use?" Maxwell asked.

Grover pressed his lips together in silence for a minute before replying.

"The one on the right at the end of the corridor. Don't think this is over. It's only just starting. I've been in contact with your boss. FBI? Investigating this crime? What a joke!"

Stella turned her face away as she passed him, fighting for calmness. She couldn't say anything now. Not until Roth had told them Grover's version. Then she'd know what she needed to do to defend herself.

But, for the time being, she was very aware how destructive Grover's interference was. Duncan was glancing from her to Maxwell suspiciously, as if he'd decided that perhaps he didn't have to cooperate with them after all, and that Grover could somehow save him from his predicament.

Hurrying down the corridor, they unlocked the interview room and Maxwell shepherded Duncan inside and sat him down on the rickety plastic chair. There was only one other chair, so Stella took it and Maxwell stood.

The room was stuffy and cramped. In its confines, Maxwell removed Duncan's cuffs. He drew his hands in front of him, rubbing his wrists meaningfully as if he was already considering how his lawyer might demand compensation for the discomfort he'd had to endure. Then he folded his arms and stared at them.

"Did you drive back from Riverside Retreat on the night of your son's party?" Maxwell snapped out.

Duncan sighed impatiently, as if this line of questioning was a huge inconvenience and waste of time.

"No. I did no such thing."

"Did you know Desiree Jardine was going to be at the party?" Maxwell probed.

"Nobody knew Desiree was going to be at the party. I asked my son about it later. He was surprised to see her arrive. He had no idea she was going to be there, and I have no idea who could have invited her."

"When did your son organize the party?"

"About a month ago. I'm not sure exactly. It was his party. Not ours."

This was sounding rehearsed. Stella thought Duncan had preplanned what he might say if he was questioned further.

"You had a motive to murder her," Maxwell said.

Now Duncan spread his arms in frustration.

"What motive, agent? Tell me what motive I had? I had a brief affair with Desiree some time ago. As my wife told you, the situation was fully resolved. There was no reason for any acrimony or ongoing grudges. Why would I have wanted to kill her, well over a year later?"

Stella pressed on, hoping to find out what had caused the earlier flare-up between husband and wife.

"Maybe because it wasn't resolved?"

Duncan sighed. "I have not communicated with Desiree recently. We didn't speak after the affair ended. You are more than welcome to check my phone records."

Stella pushed further. "You might have done it because you didn't want anyone else to know? Her wild behavior included sleeping with college students. What if she started telling them about past affairs, too? Your name would be smeared. What if it affected your work reputation?"

"Agent, you keep dragging up something that happened a year and a half ago," Duncan insisted. "If people were going to have talked, they would have done so then, not now. But nobody talked. And I own my own business. I don't answer to an employer."

"Why did you lose your temper earlier?"

"I was frustrated. As anyone would be, getting harassed again and again for no reason. It's quite clear that our local detective was right, and that this crime was committed by a random criminal."

Silence fell in the stuffy room, apart from the rattling hum of the heater pushing hot, stale air into the small space.

"Why didn't you disclose that Desiree was your ex-lover when we first interviewed you? You didn't even hint at it. In fact, reading through the transcript, we could say you purposefully omitted it," she said pointedly. "You implied you'd broken off contact with the Jardines recently, after the divorce."

"Wouldn't you have done the same?" Duncan asked. "Would you want to bring up old, irrelevant information at such a difficult time? My first priority was to protect my son and make sure we did not get unfairly accused of anything, after this catastrophe happened at our home. Yes, I might have been able to drive home and back from Riverside. Many others might also have managed to drive to our home and back again from wherever they were. Desiree was a reckless woman. I wasn't under any illusion I was the only one for her, either before or since. So why are you targeting us? Why must I be accused, when we had no idea what would happen at our son's party, or who would be there? It's beginning to feel like a witch hunt."

Now his voice was harsh with anger again.

Stella glanced at Maxwell.

They were not getting as far as they had hoped with this suspect. Fear gnawed at her belly.

"Who was the physiotherapist?" she asked, wanting to fill in the gaps in Carolyn's version while she thought of other directions that might work.

"The what?" Duncan said, looking startled.

"The physiotherapist that your wife slept with."

"Oh. You'll have to ask her that. She didn't name him, and nor did I ask," he retorted, angry again. "That is completely irrelevant. Please stop trying to make an issue out of something that is not. It's all in the past. Behind us now."

Stella nodded. "We'll be back in a minute," she said, gesturing to the door.

Outside, the corridor felt refreshingly cool and airy. Stella took a deep breath, trying to get her thoughts in order.

"We need more from him," she said.

Maxwell shrugged. "He's defensive. He's evasive. You know what they say. A lie doesn't like to be questioned."

"But we are not getting to the truth. We're caught in a loop. Both of them are insisting that the affairs are ancient history. We can't accuse him of this without some proof that he did actually make that trip back."

As she said that, Stella felt a brief certainty that she'd missed something.

Affairs. Ancient history. That was where her mind had snagged onto something.

Those words had almost fitted the puzzle together for her. Almost. Why couldn't she take that final step and draw the facts together coherently?

Perhaps it had been nothing more than her own desperate mind searching for a solution where none existed.

"We can arrest him on suspicion, and look for more evidence," Maxwell insisted.

Stella felt worried about doing that, especially in light of their current standing with the Putnam detective in charge.

"We might not get evidence. We might just get a lawyer arriving here. That will help Grover, and it will help Duncan Woods, but it won't help us."

"There has to be evidence. We can keep questioning him about his movements. Look for discrepancies in his version. Pull his call records," Maxwell insisted.

"If he's telling the truth, and he didn't have any further dealings with her since they broke it off, it won't be easy to prove," Stella warned.

"He might be lying. Maybe we need to question Carolyn again, too."

"We do, but based on these versions, he's a far stronger suspect. Carolyn said that she and Desiree were friendly afterward and there was no bad blood. She said she was thankful to her as she allowed both their affairs to be exposed."

"What I mean is that she could have mentioned her in passing to her husband," Maxwell said. "'Desiree was at the salon. Looking so good.' Or 'Desiree really has moved on after the affair, I wish you would do the same, sweetheart.' Perhaps that got under his skin for whatever reason and made him angry about what he'd done."

"There was something you said there," Stella said, grabbing his arm in excitement.

Suddenly, she saw the inconsistency in the version that the Woods had presented. The puzzle pieces slotted together at last, and she saw the missing part of the picture.

There was a massive lie, and this was where it had been hidden. Maxwell's words had helped her to realize what it was.

"I think I know what happened," she said.

"What?" Maxwell sounded startled.

"I need to check something out. You keep questioning Duncan, and make sure Grover doesn't interfere, or try to release him. I'm going back to the Woods' house because I need to speak to Clint again. Urgently."

Without explaining further, Stella turned and rushed out of the precinct.

CHAPTER TWENTY EIGHT

It was after eight p.m. when Stella knocked once again on the smart front door of the Woods' townhouse. The neighborhood was quiet, with only the occasional passing car. She saw bright windows in the house opposite, and light streaming out from upstairs in the Woods' home.

Footsteps tramped to the door, and a moment later, Clint opened it. He stared at her, looking surprised. He was wearing a U-Conn T-shirt that showed off his wide shoulders and strong, muscular arms. Stella was impressed all over again by how tall and handsome this young man was. He certainly was a son to be proud of. A son whose future and reputation any parent would want to protect.

"You're back?" he asked. "What do you want? Is everything okay? Where's my dad?" The last question was uttered more strongly, as if Clint was seriously worried about the FBI's treatment of his aggressive parent.

"Your dad is still being questioned," Stella explained. "Where's your mother?"

"She went out straight after you left. She said she was going to an emergency meeting with our lawyer."

"That's okay. I wanted to ask you something."

"Me?" Clint looked alarmed.

"Yes, you. I wanted to ask you about the night of your party."

"You do? But I already told you all about that."

"Can we go inside?" Stella asked. She wasn't going to get what she needed from Clint while he was standing in the hallway.

"Inside? Sure. Sure," Clint said again. He looked thrown by her reappearance. Now that he was home alone and without either of his parents in the house, Stella thought he also seemed more apprehensive than before.

He turned and led the way through the home.

"You want to sit in the family room?" he asked.

"Okay," Stella said, following him into a cozy lounge with a plush beige carpet and gleaming wooden rafters, where a fire burned. Couches were arranged around the fireplace.

She perched on one couch and Clint sat on another.

"I've been reviewing the accounts of the witnesses we've spoken to from the party. Based on what they said, there was a time during that night when you were in your bedroom, and Desiree was nowhere to be seen," Stella explained in a conversational tone.

Clint looked deeply uneasy at what she was saying.

"I – uh – no, it wasn't like that at all. You've got things wrong," he protested.

"I don't think so. The witnesses were clear that they didn't know where Desiree was at one stage in the late evening. And she was a social butterfly, who liked to be the center of attention. She wouldn't just disappear into the background."

"Okay," Clint said nervously. A log popped loudly in the fireplace, sending up a shower of sparks, and he jumped.

"If Desiree wasn't in the thick of things, and people noticed her absence, it was because she was with somebody. And she was with you, Clint. Wasn't she?" Stella challenged him.

Clint bit his lip.

"I – yes. Yes, she came into my room," Clint admitted in a rush. "I didn't want to say anything about it because it would make me look bad, and my parents were already so angry. But yes. When I went to my room, she came with me."

He stared at Stella, clearly in a state of high anxiety at having confessed to the truth.

But this was just the first step in the information she needed from him.

"What time was that?" she asked.

"Maybe around one, one-thirty."

"Tell me about it," Stella encouraged.

Clint's cheeks had reddened, and she didn't think it was just from the warmth of the crackling fire.

"I know what you must be thinking," he said. "You're thinking we slept together during that time."

"I'm not thinking anything," Stella corrected him. "I'm waiting for you to tell me."

"When she arrived at the party, she came straight up to me. Said how wonderful it was to be greeting the handsome host, that sort of thing. There were other guys there, I mean, everyone heard. She was flirty. Hand on my arm, stroking my face, that sort of thing."

Stella guessed that being paid so much attention to by this attractive woman had been an ego-boost for Clint. More than that, it must have made him anticipate what would happen next.

"I obviously thought – well, I thought I had a chance with her. In fact, more than a chance. A couple of my friends were joking that she was going to be my birthday present. I downplayed it of course, just laughed with them. But then, I was on my own, coming back from the bathroom, I think, and she came and found me. And I asked her to come to my room with me."

Clint stared thoughtfully at the flickering flames.

"What happened?" Stella asked.

"What do you think?" Clint retorted, and for a moment Stella heard his father clearly in his voice.

"You explain," she said.

"She – well, she ended up with her top off. We were kissing. She was telling me these things, in this husky, sexy voice. About how ripped I was, how strong I was. How hot she was for me, how this was so special for her. I mean, it was crazy."

Clint hesitated.

"Go on?" Stella said.

"Then – then, just when we were going to – well, you know, it was going to happen. And then she – it was like she backtracked. Suddenly she was pushing me back. She was sort of laughing. In a not nice way. Like she was laughing about something I didn't know."

"What did you do?"

"I was so confused. But I didn't get the chance to do anything because the next moment she'd wriggled away from me and gotten her bra back on and it was like she was really upset.

"How did you know?"

"She seemed angry. She turned away from me and she was talking in this intense voice, saying things like, 'This is it. You've gone too far. This has to stop. Jeez, where next? Are you trying to destroy everything? What a damned idiot you are.' She put her top back on and the next thing she'd left the room and banged the door shut behind her. Just like that. I thought at the time she was talking to me, and I was pretty furious and insulted. It was only the next day that I realized maybe she was speaking to herself."

"You must have been angry about that. Did you go out and look for her?"

"No!" Clint said

"Really?" Stella pushed.

"It's the truth!"

"Remember, we still have a number of witnesses to interview. If one of them claims to have seen you in the house at that time, it's proof you will have lied and there will be consequences."

She waited. Clint had the choice. He could choose to lie, or he could tell the truth. She waited for him to decide, and to see where his next words led them.

"I stayed in my room," he said firmly.

"Did you follow her afterwards?"

"No, I did not."

"Did you see where she went?"

"Honestly, no."

"Okay."

"You don't believe me. I can see you don't believe me."

"You heard what your dad said earlier. That he'd had an affair with Desiree?" Stella pushed.

"I don't want to talk about that." Clint looked mortified.

Stella thought again about why Desiree had suddenly stopped herself, become frustrated with her own behavior, and abandoned her romantic interlude with Clint. She'd realized she was about to cross a line that should not have been crossed. That her behavior was unacceptable, even for her own weakening moral code.

Desiree had finally acknowledged the slippery slope she'd been on. Drugs, affairs, an escalating pattern of destructive behavior. She'd been about to sleep with her ex-lover's son. But at that pivotal moment, she'd chosen differently.

The incident with Clint had been a turning point in Desiree's life, but sadly, it had arrived too late. Her behavior had already set into motion the events that would kill her.

Stella could theorize what had played out after Desiree left Clint's room. But she needed to confirm the background first and expose the lies.

"Were you aware at the time of the affair that your dad was sleeping with Desiree?"

"No!" His voice was high, stressed.

"No signs at all?" Stella asked.

"Alright. There were signs. I noticed that he started talking about her a lot. It was a while ago. Last year, I think. Suddenly, he was speaking about her all the time. Desiree this. Desiree that."

Stella felt victorious that Clint's words mirrored what Maxwell had said. She was getting somewhere with this.

"Maybe I should have been angry with her," Clint said, looking at her with a strange half smile. "Maybe I should have realized what was going on and stopped it."

There was silence in the warm room for a while. Just the pop and crackle of the fire.

"Did you realize?"

Clint stood up suddenly.

"Does it matter? You think I did."

"How do you feel now, knowing about it?"

"I feel what he did was wrong. Really wrong. It was a dumb thing to do. It broke my mother's heart. They've been fighting ever since."

"And you didn't know the cause?"

"I noticed the fighting. It freaked me out. It's changed our home life totally. If I'd known the cause, I would have been angry at Desiree. I would have wanted to kill her. There! I said it! Now you know!" he ended in high, agonized tones.

Stella felt a flare of triumph. She got what she needed. Now, only one more piece of information was needed to complete the picture.

But Clint was done. He stood up abruptly, as if he couldn't remain seated a moment longer.

"I can't – I can't –" he said.

He turned and rushed out of the room.

"Wait! Clint!"

Clint's footsteps thudded up the stairs. Stella ran behind him, taking them two by two as she pursued him up to the top floor and along the corridor.

He was taking refuge in his room. Stella got there just before the door slammed. She managed to get her toe in the gap and her hands on the handle.

"Clint. Clint, calm down," Stella said firmly. "Listen. Please. Listen."

He wasn't listening. He was struggling to push the door closed, and having a six-foot, well-built young man using all his force on the other side was crushing Stella's foot. The door ground against her bones, squeezing them to the point of agony in her ankle boot.

"Go! Just go!" He was breathing hard, nearly panting, as he struggled to slam the door closed, with or without her toes in the way.

Her fingers clenched around the handle; Stella fought back to keep it open.

"Clint, you need to cooperate."

The pressure didn't ease. Clint was firmly in panic mode.

"I've told you everything. There's nothing left for me to say."

"There is, Clint. I have one last question and it's important. After that, I promise I will go. I just need you to be calm and answer me truthfully."

"What?" he yelled.

"When did your mother have her hamstring injury and which physio treated it?"

Clint paused for a moment.

"You're trying to trick me again. My mother never had a hamstring injury. She never got treated by any physio," he yelled, panicked, from the other side of the three-inch gap in the door.

Stella breathed out, feeling the tension ebb from her at last. Finally, she had the information she needed. Her suspicions were correct. She knew who the killer was.

As she moved her foot, the door slammed shut. Loud music started up from inside the room, as she took out her phone to call Maxwell. He needed to get here immediately so that they could question Clint together, before his mother returned.

Then, from behind her, Stella felt rather than saw a tiny movement.

It took her a moment to realize what it was.

A thin, black cable tie, slipping over her head. A moment later, it was yanked tight from behind.

CHAPTER TWENTY NINE

Stella reacted instantly, with instincts honed by training and sharpened by fear. She dropped her phone, her hands flying to her throat. And she managed to get just one finger from her left hand under the tie.

Just one finger. It wasn't enough as the tie was yanked impossibly tight, and Stella's resisting finger was trapped, buried in her own throat.

She didn't have her gun on her. After the sting operation, there had been no time to go back to the FBI New Haven offices and retrieve it. And she couldn't speak. Couldn't shout for Clint to open up and see what was happening and get help.

Blood pounded like hammer blows in her head. Her finger-hold was giving her the tiniest thread of air. Enough to choke on, but all that meant was that she would take longer to die.

Twisting around, falling to her knees as black shadows gathered at the edges of her vision, she looked into the face of her attacker.

Carolyn Woods stared implacably back.

Bitter self-blame descended. Stella had been too slow, and she'd been careless. She hadn't been aware enough. She should have known Carolyn would anticipate that Stella might return. Carolyn had been able to get up close, thanks to the loud music, and Stella being in such a hurry to call her partner.

"Help me," Stella mouthed.

Her trapped finger was the only thing protecting her windpipe. Allowing a trickle of blood and air through. It wasn't enough for her needs. She needed air, so badly. She was being suffocated, and Carolyn was going to watch.

"I'm sorry," Carolyn murmured. "I can't let anyone know. I had to protect my son. To protect Clint. I wasn't going to let that predator have him; destroy his reputation, take his innocence. Not after she had my husband. Ruined our marriage. Shattered my life. She told me at the hair salon three weeks ago that she knew about the party, that one of the guys from U-Conn had invited her. She mentioned how much she was looking forward to it, and how fit and handsome Clint was looking. The way she spoke those words, I could have cut her throat then and there. The bitch! I knew what she wanted to do to him, and that the party would be her opportunity. I'd heard the stories about her other affairs, and her lust for younger men. I realized at that moment I had to kill her before she could tarnish my boy's reputation forever."

Stella was choking. The shadows were crowding her vision. Never had she wanted air so badly. Her body was screaming for it. Carolyn was going to let her die. Unless there was something she could do.

Stella bashed Clint's door with her foot, as hard as she could. The sole of her shoe crashed against the door and Carolyn's face contorted.

"Stop that!"

She grabbed Stella's foot and began dragging her down the tiled corridor, away from the door. Stella felt despair crush her. Clint hadn't heard, or if he had, he must have thought it was just an angry retaliation that she couldn't get in.

Now, Carolyn was going to take her away, and then move her somewhere to hide her body forever. She'd be found out, Stella was sure, but it would be too late for her.

What could she do, without the power of speech to reason with Carolyn? How could she fight her with one trapped hand and rapidly weakening limbs?

As Carolyn hauled her past a small table on the upper landing, she saw her chance.

Even though her life force felt as if it was ebbing out of her, she managed to get the strength to grab at the table.

It wasn't the table she wanted. It was the photo on it. A large, framed photo showing a happy, smiling family. Duncan, Carolyn, and Clint.

A photo protected by glass.

Stella's fingers felt weak and shaky, but she grabbed the antique table's narrow stem and tipped it to the ground with all the force she possessed.

The photo flew down, crashing onto the tiles.

The glass shattered, cracks forming a ragged spider web across the ornate frame. As Carolyn dragged her roughly toward the stairs, Stella managed to grasp the edge of the frame with her one free hand.

She scrabbled at the damaged glass, feeling it slice into her fingers, knowing she would bleed, but she needed its sharpness. Needed the life-saving edge of that ruined photo frame. It was the only thing she could use to cut the cable tie and save herself.

Terrible, constricted, gagging gasps resounded in her ears. They sounded strange, Stella thought. Then she realized she was making them.

Fear shot through her at the fact it had taken her so long to realize that. Already, her starved brain was shutting down. But her fingers, clumsy and slow and feeling as if they no longer belonged to her, managed to tease a shard of glass from the frame.

If she dropped it now, it was all over. If she dropped it now, Stella knew she would pass out within moments.

The stress and the exertion were placing even more demands for oxygen. Demands she couldn't meet. Every cell was begging for air. And then the worst happened. With a howl of rage, Carolyn saw what she was doing.

"Stop that! Stop it! I can't let you live! I can't!"

Her voice was high and panicked. Her strength seemed all out of proportion to her slender frame. It was the strength of total desperation as she made a grab for Stella's hand.

Stella tried to summon enough energy to kick her away, but she could do no more than give her a clumsy knock with her foot. She connected with her ankle, hitting the bone, and Carolyn winced and stumbled, her foot buckling under her.

"Ow! Stop that!"

Stella lifted the slice of glass to her throat. She felt its clean, sharp edge touch the torturous plastic band that was cutting off her air.

Her hand was unsteady, weak. The glass was slippery with blood. She was shaking as she moved it to the cable, terrified she would drop it before she could slice through the killing band.

And then Carolyn was on her, shrieking in panic. She swiped at Stella's hand, knocking it away from her neck. Stella clutched determinedly, pain lancing through her hand as the glass bit into her palm, praying that if she survived, she wouldn't have permanent damage to a tendon.

She had no choice, because gripping the cutting edge was her only hope.

But Carolyn was also in a rush. Also seeking to end this as soon as possible. Clearly, she'd decided that it was futile to try and get that shard away from her, and a waste of time, when there was an easier way. All she needed to do was pull the cable tie even tighter.

Breathing hard, she fumbled at Stella's nape, and Stella knew she was seeking out the end of the tie, so that she could cut off the last remaining trickle of air.

It would be all over for Stella unless she could fight her off.

Using the glass as a weapon this time, trapping the splinter between her fingers like a knuckleduster, she raised her quivering hand and punched behind her, as hard as she could.

Even though the blow was weak and clumsy, Carolyn screamed, and Stella knew her makeshift weapon had found its target.

"You cut me! Drop that now! Give it to me!"

Abandoning her efforts to tighten the tie, Carolyn grabbed Stella's wrist, squeezing hard, her fingers as cruel as claws.

Stella held onto that glass shard with all her might, cupping it in her palm as Carolyn tugged at her fist. Carolyn was not going to take it from her. She was not.

But as the dark clouds filled her vision, Stella realized with a sense of inevitability that she had no choice. Her own oxygen-starved body was going to fail her. Her strength was ebbing, and Carolyn would win.

Dimly, through the rushing noise that was starting to fill her head, Stella heard running footsteps. A familiar sound. Her partner. Maxwell, his voice loud and authoritative.

"Stop that! Let her go!"

She must be dreaming, Stella thought. There was no way Maxwell could be here.

And then she heard something so loud and final that for a moment it dissipated the clouds and there was clarity again.

The whiplash crack of a gunshot.

Screaming, her captor dropped her, and she crumpled to the floor.

There was a fight ensuing. Stella could hear cries and bangs in the background as she sprawled face down, her hand trapped underneath her, still clinging to that curved edge of glass.

All she had to do was draw it back and forth across her throat to save herself.

Just as the darkness buried her, with a final surge of strength, she pushed her throat hard against the glass edge, praying that it would slice through the tie, because she knew she had no more time left.

CHAPTER THIRTY

Maxwell's voice resounded in Stella's ears. His hands felt gentle on her shoulders as he lifted her.

"Hey, Fall. You okay?"

He called out to someone else, worry as sharp in his voice as an edge of glass.

"Her hand's covered in blood. I don't know what's going on."

Then she heard the horrified cry, from the core of his being, as the broken, bloodied cable tie fell away from her throat and landed on the floor.

Stella opened her fingers and the glass shard tumbled out. The splinter, dark with blood, skittered across the polished wooden boards.

"Okay. You're going to be okay." Maxwell gabbled, and Stella had the sense he was trying to reassure her, as much as himself.

She was winning the fight against the clouds. They were thinning, dissipating. The harsh light of the room filtered back. She was staring up at the white ceiling.

And Maxwell's face.

"We need a dressing here urgently. Have the medics arrived yet?"

Behind her, Stella heard the crackle of walkie-talkies and another voice replied, "They're on the way now. Should be a minute."

Air was rushing into her choked, burning throat. Tears streamed from her eyes, and she coughed weakly, doubling over as she gasped. It felt like a blockage was still there, but she tried to tell herself it was the injury and the pain. Nothing more, apart from her own fear.

The visceral fear of being strangled.

Stella would never forget it and knew it would haunt her nightmares forever.

Maxwell helped her onto a chair and Stella sat. Both her hands were cut. The right one badly. It was streaming blood from handling the glass shard. The left one had a small gash across the index finger where the glass had injured it as it sliced through the tie. Her throat was stinging, too.

There was another pool of blood on the floor near her. That wasn't her blood. She tried to ask if Maxwell had shot Carolyn, but all that came out of her mouth was a harsh, choking sound.

On his knees, Maxwell peered up at her, his face drawn with concern.

She tried again.

"Did – you – shoot her?" her voice didn't sound like her own at all. It was shaky and impossibly hoarse, as if her entire larynx had been bruised.

He nodded.

"In the shoulder. She's downstairs now, with two of the cops, waiting to be processed. They'll treat her wound and stop the bleeding, and as soon as they've done that, they'll come up here and help you. Then they'll take her straight to the emergency room under police guard. As soon as she's stabilized, we'll interrogate and charge her."

"How did you – get here?"

She realized that Maxwell literally had not let go of her. His left hand was slung around her, supporting her as she sat in the chair. His right hand was gently holding her right, helping to elevate it so that the bleeding would reduce faster.

"Clint," Maxwell said.

Stella's eyes widened.

"He called 911. He said he'd locked himself into his bedroom and that there was a woman threatening him and trying to break in and they must come and arrest you immediately as he feared for his life." Maxwell grimaced, with a flicker of humor in his eyes. "I imagine his mother must have put that idea into his head, but it worked for you because Clint calling the police to protect himself against the nasty FBI is what saved you. Luckily the emergency call was routed to Putnam, and I overheard it. I rushed here immediately. Got here a minute quicker than they did," Maxwell said.

That minute had made all the difference for Stella. Without a doubt, Maxwell had saved her life.

Everything had worked together, including Maxwell's arrival and her own last-ditch attempt to sever the cable tie. She'd had only a second or two left before Carolyn would have won.

Maxwell's face was full of questions, and she knew he was wondering how she'd figured it out.

Even though it hurt as if the glass shard itself was in her throat, Stella did her best to explain, pushing through the pain of her injured voice box.

"I realized that Carolyn was lying. It clued me in up at the police station, when Duncan refused to tell us who she'd had her affair with," Stella began, speaking slowly in her cracked, ragged voice. "I thought Duncan was just being obstructive. But there was a difference in the way he spoke when we asked him about that. And I thought back to how he'd shouted at her when we were in the house, after she gave that story."

This was all taking a long time to tell, word by painful word. Stella wished she could get the explanation out faster from her injured throat.

"He was freaking out that she was lying?" Maxwell asked.

"Not just lying. She was inventing an entire alternative scenario on the fly, including admitting to two affairs that never actually happened. But she had to. If she didn't make the lie big enough, we weren't going to go away."

Maxwell nodded, and she knew he was remembering the way that Carolyn Woods had spilled out the detailed story of affairs and reconciliation in order to skillfully defuse their suspicion, saying that she'd been the one who had started it, and that she'd forgiven Desiree since.

"But when we checked her version with him, Duncan couldn't give us a name because his wife's story was false, and this was the first time he'd heard it. All he could say was that he didn't know."

"Yes. That seemed strange to me. I thought he was stonewalling."

"So did I, at first. That's why I went to confirm with Clint. He said his parents had been fighting ever since the affair, which contradicted Carolyn's version. He also told me his mother never had a hamstring injury, which meant it was all a fake story. Unfortunately, as he said that, she was already behind me. She must have come back inside and heard him shouting. She surprised me. She got the cable tie around my neck before I could stop her."

"Hell!" Maxwell uttered in heartfelt tones.

He paused for a while, thinking hard.

"Why do you think she killed Desiree? Because Desiree was going to sleep with her son as well as her husband and she couldn't handle it?" Maxwell asked.

Stella recalled the conversation she'd had with the hesitant, embarrassed Clint.

"That's why. But the irony is that Desiree didn't sleep with Clint. She stopped herself and got angry with her own behavior and walked out on him. I guess it was a tipping point. She rethought her life, and turned away from the path she'd been on, but it came too late."

Maxwell nodded solemnly, taking in the tragedy of Desiree's unnecessary death.

Stella thought again about the complex layers of the person Desiree had been.

An adventurous person. Immoral for sure. She'd cheated on her husband. She had brief hookups with younger men. She'd used hard drugs. But she'd been a good and protective mother, and a dedicated professional in her job. She'd never exposed her son to her behavior. And when it came down to it, she'd realized her destructive path, and tried to change who she was becoming.

Unfortunately, the woman who'd taken her life had possessed no boundaries. She'd cared only about protecting her son, and then herself.

She'd cunningly preplanned the murder, knowing that being at Riverside Retreat would give her the perfect alibi as well as the ideal opportunity to drive back. Stella was sure she'd disguised herself, most probably pulling on a hooded top and shades so that nobody would recognize her as she crept into her own home.

Then it was only a matter of finding Desiree.

Stella remembered that snippet of conversation that Ollie had overheard.

"We must talk."

"Oh, hey! Yes, we must!"

That was Desiree, surprise in her voice, recognizing the killer. Carolyn would then have suggested they walk through the trashed house and into her bedroom.

Most probably she hadn't wasted any time. Stella guessed she'd said a polite, "After you," and got that noose around Desiree's neck as soon as she'd stepped through the door.

Then, after she'd stashed Desiree's body in the tub, she'd opened the sliding door and made her escape out of the bedroom, walking calmly across the sweeping lawns back to the road where she'd left her car. A quick drive back, and she thought she'd committed the perfect crime.

Of course, there had been the matter of the police investigation, but thinking it through, Stella guessed that Carolyn Woods had felt she was in safe hands. She must have known that the detective would be open to persuasion in whatever form it took to protect the reputation of her 'fine young man' and would ensure that the investigation did not focus on Clint or his family.

Carolyn must have thought she was home and dry, but then in a shocking twist of fate, Grover had been away at a funeral and his assistant had quite rightly called in the FBI – a move that Grover himself would never have made. Stella could imagine how horrified Carolyn must have been on hearing this bombshell. No wonder she'd looked so visibly nervous when Stella and Maxwell had knocked at their door. And no wonder Grover had been so angry about it.

That reminded Stella there was still an issue with Grover. She'd solved the case, but not the rest of the trouble she was in, and tomorrow morning, she would have to face the consequences.

CHAPTER THIRTY ONE

It was after ten p.m. when Maxwell dropped Stella at home. She'd taken him up on the offer of the ride to save her hand. It needed to heal fast, and that meant she'd be using cabs for a while.

"You sure you're going to be all right?" he asked, glancing at her bandaged hand.

"I'm sure. It's not feeling too sore," Stella lied.

The medics had neatly stitched up the deep gash, and dressed her other minor wounds, including a few slices on both her hands and a deep gash in her neck. Her neck was bruised and swollen from the constriction of the cable tie. The hand still throbbed, and Stella knew it would probably do so for a few days. She'd be off fieldwork until her injuries had fully healed. That meant a couple of weeks in the New Haven back office.

With the money laundering case now fully wrapped up, Stella guessed she might end up bumping into Carrie again.

Tomorrow morning was going to be her day of reckoning with Roth. He'd said so in a terse message to her a few minutes ago. The words were etched in Stella's mind.

"Well done for solving the case. Good work. Hope your injury is feeling better soon. We need to discuss other matters urgently. My office, 6.30 a.m. tomorrow."

Stella felt sick with nerves when she thought of the upcoming meeting.

"You sure you're okay?" Maxwell asked her, sounding more concerned now. "You're looking very worried."

Stella shrugged. She was not going to allow Maxwell to get embroiled in what was, one hundred percent, a situation of her own making.

"It's been a very long day," she said wryly.

"You're telling me," Maxwell said in heartfelt tones. "You want to head out for a drink or something to wind down?"

For a moment, Stella was tempted to say yes. A drink with Maxwell and winding down felt like the perfect conclusion to this long, stressful day, and a celebration that they'd solved the case.

But reluctantly, she shook her head, thinking of the morning meeting and that she needed to be rested for it. It could mean anything, most likely a major setback to her career. There would definitely be negative consequences that she'd have to handle.

"Tomorrow night, instead?" she said. "I'm pretty shattered tonight and have to get an early start." She decided not to mention the meeting with Roth. She didn't want to worry Maxwell, or worse still, have him try to shoulder some of the blame for what would happen.

Maxwell grinned wryly. "Yeah. I hear you. Being on admin duty always makes me want to lie down."

Stella laughed, feeling her nervousness about the morning meeting ease slightly. She loved watching Maxwell when those rare grins lit up his face. She liked the way his dark eyes narrowed mischievously, the way the smile softened the hard, angular planes of his features.

"And, of course, you just got stitched up." Gently, he touched her wrist above the bandage. The warm pressure of his fingers on her skin made Stella feel momentarily dizzy.

"So it's a date tomorrow night, then?" he asked, and as she nodded in agreement, his emphasis on the word made her realize that Maxwell meant a date in every sense.

With a skip of her heart, Stella saw that Maxwell was looking at her closely, and the expression in his eyes was no longer humor but something else. Something more serious and more intense. The attraction between them could not be denied. It was growing. They were becoming closer in every sense. During this dangerous, frustrating and complicated case, each of them had saved the other's life.

Stella was learning that such an action created deep bonds. And that was over and above the physical spark that she was having more and more difficulty controlling.

"I was so damned worried about you. I'm so glad you're okay."

After a long moment, Maxwell let go of her wrist. He climbed out and walked around to open Stella's door.

She scrambled clumsily out, gripping her purse in her left hand and holding her throbbing, bandaged right hand out to the side.

Maxwell took her purse from her and grasped her arm helpfully.

Stella stumbled over a bump in the sidewalk, and he held onto her tighter.

"Sorry," she said, feeling awkward beyond words, but it was more because of Maxwell's presence close beside her, than because of her injuries.

"Stella," he said, his voice filled with concern. "Sorry for what?"

His face was close to hers as he turned to her.

Stella didn't know. Perhaps there was no reason to fight this any longer, she thought. She closed her eyes, feeling swept away by the attraction that flooded her. Maxwell's lips touched hers and her stomach flip-flopped as they kissed.

This was it, she thought, there was no going back. Here, standing on the sidewalk on a cold winter night, was the place where she had decided her life would change and she was ready to trust again. For a few moments, Stella gave herself up to the sensations, the feel of Maxwell's lips on hers, his hands cupping her waist, a roughness in his breathing that had not been there before.

"Wow, Stella," he whispered when they moved away from each other.

Stella's head felt light. Her knees felt weak. For those few intense moments, she'd forgotten entirely about her injured hand.

She lifted her left hand and stroked his face, letting her fingers explore those hard planes, a trace of stubble rough against her fingertips and his skin soft underneath.

Then she stepped back and took her purse from him.

"Good night," she said.

She turned and walked away, feeling as if something momentous had happened, something that would change her life going forward. She headed to the elevator feeling as if she was in a dream, reliving every moment of that amazing kiss, feeling hope bloom inside her.

The elevator pinged at the same time her phone did. She had an incoming message.

As the elevator swooped its way up to her floor, Stella read the message.

It was from Jeff, the helpful neighbor she'd met in Ouray, Colorado.

"Hey Stella. I've asked about your dad and found something that might help."

Her heart quickening, Stella scrolled quickly down through the rest of the text.

"Ruth, who owns the co-op, says he still has his old PO box in town. The rental gets paid every year and she told me the box is checked by someone. It's mostly just flyers and pamphlets and junk mail that goes in there, but every so often, every few months, she sees it

has been emptied. Here's her number if you want to ask her anything more."

Stella looked up, realizing in shock that the elevator doors were already open on her floor. She hadn't even noticed. She walked out, buoyed by hope as she considered what this might mean.

It meant her father was still alive and he was still retaining that one connection with the town. Perhaps he got important letters sent there.

A box that was checked could mean a solid lead to her father at last.

She unlocked the apartment door, feeling overwhelmed with excitement at this news. There was no way she could sleep now. She needed to process this information for a while, and plan how she was going to use it.

How Stella wished she'd taken Maxwell up on his offer of a drink. She wished she could talk to him about this. She'd been an idiot to have declined the invitation. Especially after that brief, intense kiss that had changed the landscape between them.

Well, it was never too late, Stella thought. She could catch a cab and meet him at his place. They could go for that drink. She could tell him the news.

Quickly, Stella called a cab. Working awkwardly with her sore, stitched hands, she changed her top and refreshed her lipstick. She undid her braid, and loosened her hair with the fingertips of her left hand.

She rushed outside just as the cab pulled up.

As soon as she was in, she messaged him left-handedly.

"I changed my mind. I'm on my way to you. Let's have that drink!"

She'd been to Maxwell's place once before, when he'd detoured there to pick up jackets for them on a day that had turned gray and rainy. It was a light, bright, modern apartment on the top floor of a building that overlooked the ocean. It was only a ten-minute drive from her place, and Stella spent the time in happy anticipation of what would follow.

*

It was only when the cab pulled up outside the apartment block that she realized Maxwell hadn't texted her back. In fact, he hadn't even read the message yet.

Stella climbed out, thinking wryly that she'd been the one pleading tiredness when in fact Maxwell must have been so drained by the day's events that he'd gotten straight into the shower without checking his phone.

She felt a flicker of uncertainty that he might not want her arriving at his front door and that he'd now decided on a peaceful evening. Oh, well, she thought. Even if she hadn't thought this through, she was here now.

She took the elevator up to the top floor and headed to his apartment, number three.

As she reached it, she saw the door was partway open. Light streamed out, and she heard voices inside. She hesitated because this didn't sound like the television. It sounded like Maxwell himself.

Wondering what was going on, Stella tapped on the half-open door and then stepped into the apartment.

Beyond the small hallway, in the bright, modern lounge, Maxwell sat on the couch, side by side with a woman Stella had never seen before. She was blond, and looked to be around Stella's age, wearing a bright blue, sparkly top that clung to her figure, showing off her curves and her slender waist. Their heads were close together, and she brushed her hair back from her face as they spoke, twining her fingers through a thick, sandy lock.

Stella stared, starting to feel sick inside. Who was this woman? Why was she here, in his apartment, at this hour? She felt totally confused. Was she a neighbor, a friend? Somehow, from the way she was interacting with him, sitting so close and playing with her hair, Stella didn't think so.

Then the blonde saw Stella.

"Rick, who's this?" she asked, sounding puzzled.

Maxwell looked up and saw her. The horror that filled his face told Stella more than she ever wanted to know.

He scrambled to his feet immediately.

"Am I interrupting something? You haven't read my message," Stella said.

Her voice didn't even sound like her own. It was harsh and shaky. Her unbandaged hand felt icy cold.

"I – I – Fall, I'm sorry," Maxwell stammered out.

Stella felt as if he'd stabbed her in the heart. At this moment, he'd chosen to call her by her last name, the formal address they used at work. Just ten minutes ago, he'd been whispering 'Stella' as he kissed her. Now, she was Fall.

"Oh, this is your work partner?" the blonde said, realization dawning in her voice. "I'd better go. We'll speak later," she said to him meaningfully.

She turned and walked out. Stella stepped aside as she sashayed past. She was immaculately made up, with long false eyelashes that accentuated her green eyes. Her top was decorated in Swarovski crystals and looked expensive. She was confident and beautiful, and, to Stella's utter shock, she picked up the gleam of gold and the glint of a bright jewel on the third finger of her left hand.

"Nice to meet you." She gave Stella a perfunctory smile as she passed, as if Stella meant nothing in her life and was of no importance. Not a threat, not even a blip on her radar.

Her heels clicked as she headed out of sight but the light, floral tinge of her scent lingered, flavoring the air of the spacious apartment.

"What is going on?" Stella asked, turning back to Maxwell. She knew what was going on. It wasn't difficult to figure out. She guessed the reason she was asking was out of a vain hope that things were somehow going to be different from what she feared.

Looking stressed, he put down his phone and she guessed that too late, he'd read her message.

"That's Brigitte," he said. His voice didn't sound the same either anymore. It was terse and unhappy. This spelled bad news, Stella knew. Very, very bad news.

"Who's Brigitte?" she asked.

"She's my wife," Maxwell said heavily. He wasn't looking at Stella. He was staring at the floor instead.

"Your… wife?" Stella confirmed.

Maxwell nodded.

"Not your ex?" Now that the shock was dissipating, she felt rage building, as thick and heavy as storm clouds. She wasn't angry at Maxwell. She was angry at herself. How could she have been such an idiot as to trust again? She should have known better.

"Not my ex. We're not yet divorced. We're separated. We've been separated nearly two years. I'm so sorry. I've become so used to living alone, in limbo. I should have told you before, when you asked. Since then, the time never seemed right."

Stella remembered the first time she'd asked him about his background, he'd admitted – sort of – to a romantic break-up that had propelled him into a new career with the FBI. But he'd said nothing about it since then. Nothing about the fact that it hadn't, in fact, been a real break-up and that he was still married to her!

Would he ever have told her? Or was he never intending to? How could she trust him again, she agonized.

"Brigitte clearly wants to change that, if she's pitching up at your apartment late at night."

Maxwell gave another reluctant nod.

"She does, yes," he admitted.

"Why didn't you tell me any of this before – before –" Stella couldn't get the words out. She found herself unable to even think about the kiss they'd shared earlier. That moment, that had felt like a beginning, full of promise and excitement, now seemed like a mockery.

"You're so dumb, Stella, you'll believe anything. Wake up and realize what the world is all about. It's not the place you want it to be. It's harsh and cruel and filled with disappointments."

Her mother's furious words for once rang true in Stella's mind.

"Please understand," Maxwell fumbled. "It's not a simple situation."

"It seems pretty simple to me. You're not divorced. You're still married. And you didn't feel it necessary to mention that fact to me?" Stella's voice rose incredulously.

"She wants to get back together. We had a serious talk about it in August. Since then, I've been backing off and she's been pushing for it."

"Why's that?" Stella demanded.

Now, finally, Maxwell met her eyes.

"Because of you! Because I met you. And now I've landed in an impossible situation because I told Brigitte – I promised her – that we'd try again, but I don't want to. So I've been feeling wretched. That I'm stuck in a problem of my own making, and my decision is going to end up causing hurt and disappointment, and more. It's complicated."

He could have discussed it with her. She'd told him her private feelings and put her shameful secrets on the table. He'd chosen not to do the same and that left Stella feeling utterly betrayed.

"I'll tell you what," Stella spat the words out. "I'm going to make it easy for you. Try again with her, Maxwell. Give it your all. Because it's over between you and me. I don't want anything to do with you, ever."

There was more she wanted to say. Stella felt appalled by how readily the vicious insults bubbled to the surface. How she wanted to scream that he was a cheat and a liar, a false person who'd abused her trust. She knew she could wound him, lacerate him, destroy him with words. She could use them to make sure he never came near her and had the chance to hurt her again.

She clamped her mouth shut with an effort. Even though the temptation to let rip, to say how she felt, burned inside her, she was not going to let herself become like Rhonda Fall.

In silence, and without saying another word, she turned and walked away.

"Stella! Wait!" he called, his voice ragged.

But she didn't wait. She didn't even hesitate. She marched around the corner without looking back.

CHAPTER THIRTY TWO

The next morning, at six-fifteen a.m., Stella arrived for her meeting with Roth. The hour was so early that even the New Haven office was still waking. She picked up the distant sound of vacuums and floor polishers. The night shift team were signing out and handing over. A few people were arriving, heading purposefully to their offices because urgent assignments were waiting.

Each tramp of footsteps on the tiled floor represented a small addition to the collective energy the day would bring, Stella thought.

She had barely slept. Her hand was on fire, swollen and throbbing. Stella knew it was a sign of healing. The pain, though excruciating, was at least a distraction from the emotional agony she felt, which was all but unbearable.

The awful moments of yesterday played and replayed in her head. She couldn't erase them. The moment she'd realized Maxwell's betrayal. How could he have done that?

Self-blame and anger warred for priority in her mind. With a huge effort, Stella suppressed them both as she headed down the corridor to Roth's offices.

Now was not the time to wallow in emotion. She was in trouble and had to face the consequences alone. At least she was now prepared for whatever outcome her reckless words had caused.

If she had to leave New Haven and transfer elsewhere, so be it, Stella thought. She couldn't pretend she would be heartbroken by the move and could regard it as a new opportunity and a chance to rebuild.

She just wouldn't make the mistake of falling in love with a co-worker again, she resolved bitterly.

Roth was an early bird and even though Stella had arrived fifteen minutes before the scheduled meeting time, he rushed in only a minute later.

"You're here already? Good. Come through," he told her.

She felt even more nervous as she picked up on Roth's formal tone. She had no idea what it meant but she feared it would be the worst news.

Roth was a morning coffee addict and hadn't even suggested they get a cup. That, too, was significant – and not in a good way, Stella worried.

She sat opposite him, waiting to hear exactly how bad the trouble was that she'd landed herself in.

"This is difficult for me to say, Fall," he said in a hard voice, pulling out a chair on the other side of his desk and sitting down.

Stella waited. Her heart was hammering so loudly she was sure Roth could hear it. Her mouth was dry, and she felt intensely nauseous. Please, don't let it be a lawsuit, she thought. Not a lawsuit. She couldn't afford it and it would reflect so badly on the FBI. It wouldn't be right for her to ask for Roth's help in opposing a problem that she had personally caused.

Stella felt filled with shame as she waited for Roth to explain the fallout that had occurred as a result of her actions.

It would be difficult to pick herself up again from wherever this landed her. But even in her despair, Stella resolved she would do it. She would not let this crush her. She'd come out fighting. No matter what it took.

Roth steepled his fingers and regarded her for a few more moments.

"I have always tried to lead by example. But yesterday, I failed. I owe you a huge apology," he said.

The breath whooshed out of Stella. She literally rocked back in her chair as she stared at him.

"What?" she faltered.

He nodded.

"I did exactly what I have repeatedly advised you never to do. I jumped to conclusions based on insufficient evidence, and without having all the facts available

"How – how is that possible?" Stella asked.

"Yesterday, Detective Grover called me in a fury. He said that at lunch time, while he was out of the Putnam police precinct, a female FBI agent arrived and demanded to look through the old case files. The sergeant on duty was apparently reassured of her credentials and convinced by her request and let her go through to the back office without questioning her."

What was going on, Stella wondered. When would Roth start mentioning the defamatory comments that she'd made?

"It wasn't me," she said. "I don't know who it could have been, but it must have been in connection with something different and unrelated."

Roth nodded. "I assumed it was, without confirming properly with you. Grover was absolutely livid, and he called me, demanding that the agents on the Jardine case stop prying into unrelated matters. I believed you were the instigator, and that you were deviating from your mandate, while knowing that we needed to focus all our attention on the active case, and also knowing that you were expected to manage the political situation with Grover. So yes, I intended, up until late yesterday evening, to give you a serious disciplinary talk as a result. And then I realized I was wrong, and it wasn't you."

The way Roth was speaking, he'd found this out because he'd discovered who it was. And as Stella reached the shocked conclusion for herself, Roth confirmed it.

"Agent Carrie Potts went to Putnam. She left the New Haven office at noon after pulling an all-nighter wrapping up her duties in the money laundering case. Having handed in her report, she then drove straight there."

"Why?" Stella asked. She felt utterly blindsided by this revelation. She'd been certain all along that Carrie was planning to stab her in the back, but she'd been focused on obtaining old case files. Stella couldn't understand it.

"Apparently, Potts was very invested in the outcome of the Jardine case. She told me yesterday evening that you'd mentioned Grover had said the case would go cold, and that there had been two other similar cases that had never been solved, while he'd been in charge."

Stella felt gooseflesh prickle up and down her spine.

"Potts realized it would be difficult for you to pull the files as Grover was being obstructive," Roth continued. "But she thought the information in them could possibly be useful – not for solving the case, but for proving that Grover himself was incompetent, biased, and possibly corrupt."

Stella now felt absolutely stunned. That had been a brilliant and daring move on Carrie's part. She couldn't believe that Carrie had gone out of her way, and exposed herself to a lot of potential trouble, in order to help Grover get what he deserved.

"She presented me with her report on the files yesterday evening, after hearing that the current case had been solved."

"What are the two previous cases?" Stella asked.

"Both involved student parties. In the first, fifteen years ago, a young female backpacker was found dead in the garden. She'd been assaulted and beaten up. Potts showed me the case file and it was pretty obvious that someone from the large house party must have been the perpetrator. But yet, nobody was ever arrested. Grover blamed it on a random vagrant. He protected the local boys. There's no evidence how far the investigation went or if he was paid off. But then, five years later, a similar thing happened."

"What?" Stella asked.

"There was an overnight camp where college students arrived from the local area. Things got wild and a woman was found suffocated with a pillow. She was a student from Massachusetts, who'd recently lost her parents in a car crash. Again, not much effort was put into finding out who committed the crime, and it grew cold. Again, it's obvious that Grover was incentivized to protect the locals."

"Can anything be done?" Stella asked, horrified.

"We're looking into it and will take action," Roth said. "But in the meantime, accept my sincere apologies. I know I was busy and stressed out, but it won't happen again."

"Thank you, Roth. I appreciate the apology. It's accepted in full. I understand."

Stella felt weak with relief and shock. Grover's corruption would be scrutinized. And Carrie – well, in a move that was one of the biggest shocks she'd ever had, Carrie had chosen not to destroy her with the information she possessed and had actually been working on her side.

Stella knew it had been nothing personal and that it was because Carrie's mother was so invested in the outcome of the Jardine case. But even so, Stella wondered whether this might represent a possibility – just a slim chance – that they might be able to cooperate together without actual conflict one day.

Spurred on by that hope, Stella found herself voicing a request that didn't even seem to relate to her.

"Roth, I feel that Potts and I have not had the chance to gel properly. I feel there's been competition between us rather than cooperation."

"Yes," he agreed. "I've picked that up, too."

Stella took a deep breath. "I'd like this to change. Now's a good time. Could I be partnered with Carrie Potts for a while?"

As she said the words, she felt flattened by shock. What had she just asked for? What had she just done? Her request was reckless. And yet, it represented an escape route from an impossible situation.

"You've been working well with Maxwell," Roth said doubtfully. The mention of his name sent a spear into Stella's heart.

"It was just an idea," she said casually, as if it didn't mean everything to her. She didn't want Roth to know that she'd been idiotic enough to fall for him. "I've worked very well with Maxwell. But in my career, I'm going to need to be partnered with different people. Some I'll get on with and some I won't. I might as well start figuring out how to deal with the difficult partnerships earlier."

Roth nodded. "True. True. Okay, I like your reasoning and I'll see what I can do. And now, I'd better go and grab a coffee for us. After you've signed off the rest of the paperwork on the Jardine case, you can go home. You need to rest up, so I'm giving you three days off."

With a quick grin, he got up and hurried out.

Stella shook her head, still feeling astonished by what had happened. She'd never dreamed Roth would end up apologizing to her. Never.

She wasn't going to rest up, though. She was going to start the process of finding out more about her father's disappearance. This would be her chance to make a connection with the Kansas precinct, to discover what cases he was working on at the time, and to get in touch with Ruth, who owned the co-op in Ouray where the PO boxes were.

But, when Roth came back in with the coffees, his face was serious again.

"Fall, there's one more thing I need to tell you. A report came in early today. When I saw it, I knew I needed to share it with you urgently."

"What?" Stella said, feeling a twinge of doubt. From Roth's tone, and the look on his face, this didn't sound positive.

"There was a verdict yesterday afternoon on the Marshall trafficking case. Cecilia Marshall was found guilty on all counts. She was sentenced to ten years in jail."

As Stella drew in a gasp of horror, Roth continued.

"She had a breakdown last night. She overdosed on sleeping pills and alcohol and was declared dead in the small hours of the morning. I know you played a role in bringing her to book. The officer who attended the death said that her husband was beside himself. He was vowing that he would get revenge. They're a powerful family, so tread carefully for the next while, and watch your back," Roth warned.

Stella stared at him wordlessly. As a result of her intervention, and her exposure of the family's crimes, there had been an actual suicide.

Gordon was already promising revenge, and Stella knew she would be his prime target. Worse still, she'd just severed ties with the partner who would protect her, and had requested Carrie, who knew the Marshalls, and would willingly throw her to the wolves.

Now, Gordon would be coming after her, seeking to destroy her using every resource he had.

NOW AVAILABLE FOR PRE-ORDER!

HIS OTHER LIFE

(A Stella Fall Psychological Suspense Thriller—Book 5)

A father is found dead in a wealthy suburb, and on the surface, his life looks perfect. But as Stella digs deeper she realizes the victim was hiding a secret life—and it may be the key to finding the killer.

HIS OTHER LIFE is book #5 in a new psychological suspense series by debut author Ava Strong, which begins with HIS OTHER WIFE (Book #1).

To all appearances, the victim hit all the checkmarks of a successful life, working for an exclusive finance firm, a member of an exclusive yacht club, having the perfect house in suburbia, a wife, two kids and a picket fence. But as FBI special agent Stella Fall goes deeper down the rabbit hole of evidence, she soon realizes he wasn't as much of a good guy as he pretended to be. What was he really up to on Dad's Night Out? On Dad's weekends away? At his firm?

Something isn't adding up. But time is running out, and it's up to Stella to put the pieces together.

Can she unravel the twisted puzzle in time to stop the murderer?

A fast-paced psychological suspense thriller with unforgettable characters and heart-pounding suspense, HIS OTHER LIFE is book #5 in a riveting new series that will leave you turning pages late into the night.

Book #6—HIS OTHER TRUTH—is also available.

Ava Strong

Debut author Ava Strong is author of the REMI LAURENT mystery series, comprising six books (and counting); of the ILSE BECK mystery series, comprising seven books (and counting); and of the STELLA FALL psychological suspense thriller series, comprising six books (and counting).

An avid reader and lifelong fan of the mystery and thriller genres, Ava loves to hear from you, so please feel free to visit www.avastrongauthor.com to learn more and stay in touch.

BOOKS BY AVA STRONG

REMI LAURENT FBI SUSPENSE THRILLER
THE DEATH CODE (Book #1)
THE MURDER CODE (Book #2)
THE MALICE CODE (Book #3)
THE VENGEANCE CODE (Book #4)
THE DECEPTION CODE (Book #5)
THE SEDUCTION CODE (Book #6)

ILSE BECK FBI SUSPENSE THRILLER
NOT LIKE US (Book #1)
NOT LIKE HE SEEMED (Book #2)
NOT LIKE YESTERDAY (Book #3)
NOT LIKE THIS (Book #4)
NOT LIKE SHE THOUGHT (Book #5)
NOT LIKE BEFORE (Book #6)
NOT LIKE NORMAL (Book #7)

STELLA FALL PSYCHOLOGICAL SUSPENSE THRILLER
HIS OTHER WIFE (Book #1)
HIS OTHER LIE (Book #2)
HIS OTHER SECRET (Book #3)
HIS OTHER MISTRESS (Book #4)
HIS OTHER LIFE (Book #5)
HIS OTHER TRUTH (Book #6)

www.ingramcontent.com/pod-product-compliance
Lightning Source LLC
Chambersburg PA
CBHW030616310726
48979CB00003B/744

9781094393544